In the Realm of
Mist and Mercy

For Addison and Aedan

MIST AND MERCY
BOOK 1

In the Realm of
Mist and Mercy

by
Susan A. Howard

Our Sunday Visitor
www.osv.com

Part I

GATHERING MIST

1

In the Wood

THE regal, ten-point stag lifted his head and swiveled his ears in Waljan's direction. The young hunter paused, every muscle locked. Having drawn back the creaking sinew of his bow, his fingers ached against the tension. He waited for the animal to relax. Every minute sound—a sudden scurry, a rustle, or a chirp—amplified in the unseasonably foggy air. The stag returned to his midday meal, and Waljan took aim.

It had to be a fatal shot. Waljan preferred hunger to chasing a frantic, tortured deer through the woods. His arm quivered. Concentrate, he thought. Suddenly, the stag raised his head and looked directly at Waljan.

In an instant, an unseen arrow whistled through the air and thrust itself high in the trunk of a nearby ash tree. The stag bolted and disappeared. By the time Waljan realized what had happened, his own arrow had lodged deep into the soil at his feet. He was lucky he still had all his toes.

"You nearly had him, Boy!" Haden said to his apprentice in encouragement as well as reproof.

"I did have him, Sir ... if it weren't for that ... Pe-nel-o-peeeee! I know that's you!" Waljan yelled into the surrounding wood.

"You hesitated," Haden insisted as he wrested the arrow from the ground. "He was on to you, Boy, but you had time to get off a shot."

"But Sir, if I had been any quieter, I wouldn't have been here at all!"

"Well, you do tend to breathe in sharply when you draw the bow . . . like you're about to jump into ice-cold water. That stag has a fine set of ears."

"Still, I had plenty of time. Penelope stole my kill."

"No one stole anything, Boy. That shot was high. And Penelope doesn't miss."

"Exactly. I'm telling you, Sir. It was Penelope, and she missed on purpose."

"Of course I did!" A bubbly voice sprang from the brush, followed by its owner. Bits of bark and dried leaves poked out from her matted bronze curls. Her freckled cheeks and nose hid behind smudges of black soot, and rich, brown soil-caked under her fingernails.

"Those antlers were never meant to hang on someone's wall," Penelope declared. "Besides, the meat would have been way too tough even for your stew, Waljan."

"And who made you the game warden, Penelope Longbow?" Waljan asked testily.

"Oh, don't be such a baby," Penelope scolded, her overly large chestnut eyes flashing.

"Never mind, Waljan," said Haden. "We have more than enough rabbit for tonight. And as for you, young lady, does your brother know you're out here alone? Waljan's stray arrows are the least of your worries in the Wood."

The boy grimaced.

"Yes, Cullie knows I'm here. We just shot and dressed a doe on the other side of Promise Rock. I went to gather some roots and spotted that beauty grazing. I'd been watching him for some time.

"You look like it," Haden said, as he brushed a disoriented beetle off her shoulder.

"I was thinking of taking a splash in the stream. Can Waljan come with me, Mr. Hunter?"

"Why would I want to come with you after you stole my deer?" Waljan interjected.

"First of all, it isn't your deer. Secondly, if you want to kill something so badly, I am sure you will get another chance. But you don't have to come. I can go by myself."

"Not if I have any say about it," Haden said. "If something ever happened to you, your brother would never forgive me. And I wouldn't blame him."

"Yeah, you'd probably fall in and drown," Waljan teased.

"Probably. And it would be on your head," she retorted.

"Fine. I'll go with you. But you owe me a stag."

"I do not!" Penelope laughed, and the two started toward the stream, bickering back and forth.

"Now wait just a minute, you two," Haden objected. "Waljan and I have to be headed home, and I think you've been gone long enough, young lady. We'll walk you back to Culbert."

The pair grumbled and moaned, but soon after resumed their competitive banter as they followed Haden through Mortwood's lush understory.

The Wood lay just beyond civilization in the dark and brooding land of Mortania. Though beautiful and full of life, the forest was wild and dangerous. Many things, real and imagined, lurked there. But to Haden Hunter and his young, sandy-haired apprentice Waljan Woodland, it was home.

Haden found Waljan as an infant, bellowing in the damp morning air from inside a tree hollow. The baby was cold and hungry, but sheltered. Few people wandered that part of the Wood, but many other predators did. Haden examined the ground for tracks and scanned the area. He found no one to claim the child. So, he took the boy in and tended to him as best an old bachelor could.

Not too many months before, Waljan's mother, Alicia, would not have imagined abandoning her little one. She and her husband, Aimas, had started their life together in a small woodland hut, a half-day beyond the city of Mortinburg. Their lives were simple. Having few opportunities for work, the couple gathered, cut, and bundled firewood for sale in the marketplace. The hard work brought very little money, but they made do and were happy.

After Waljan was born, Alicia became very sick and could no longer help her husband prepare the loads for sale. Just caring for the baby was enough to sap her energy, and her weakness put a greater strain on Aimas as the sole provider for the family.

"He's ruined you!" Aimas snapped one evening as he came in for supper.

"No, my dear, don't let your fear pit you against your own son. Don't worry about me; I will be fine. Waljan is helpless now, but in a few short years he will be a great benefit to you."

Aimas softened. "I am just tired," he said. "I'll take my meal outside. I have work yet to finish before I leave for town in the morning."

One day, Alicia collapsed into Aimas's arms with a fever so

intensely hot that it frightened the sturdy young husband out of his hardened manner. He gently placed his muttering wife on the bed and anxiously spread damp rags across her forehead. Waljan cooed from his cradle, and Aimas glared at him.

"You! You are the reason she is so sick!" he said through desperate tears.

Several days passed before Alicia's fever finally broke and Aimas decided a day of rest for the whole family was long overdue. He took Alicia and Waljan, whom the couple called "Wally," to the river to fish and pick berries. The warmth of midday coaxed from the brambles a rich sweetness that hung in the summer air. As the river slipped quietly away through the woods, the couple dropped their baskets under a shade tree and spread a moth-eaten blanket over the clover.

No sooner had they settled in, than a figure appeared from behind a stand of trees.

Tall and fit, with sharp features and dark, penetrating eyes, the man tipped his black silk hat and bowed low with a gloved hand solemnly at his chest. In the crook of his arm, he held an elegant, ebony walking stick topped with a silver goat skull.

"Asmodeus, at your service," he announced, handing Alicia a calling card. She giggled at his formality. Aimas just stared.

The man tossed his walking stick aside and nestled between the couple, leaning back on one elbow as if he had been invited to join them. Aimas found the man's boldness strangely amusing. But Alicia grew nervous. His attire and manners made her too aware of her own shabby poverty.

"Well," Aimas said to the man, "you've added spark to an otherwise ordinary day. You must be new to Mortwood. My name is Aimas, and this is my wife, Alicia."

"No, and I know.," Asmodeus replied. "Your expression suggests I should explain. No, I am not new to the Wood, but to one of those quaint Mortanian villages . . . Smithtown or something. This dreary wood is not suited for a man of my breeding. And I know who you are. I have been watching you."

Aimas and Alicia were not sure how to feel about this last statement. On the one hand, it was flattering that such a man would find interest in a poor family from the Wood. Yet the same interest seemed threatening as well. Their discomfort must have been obvious for Asmodeus burst out in protest.

"Oh my! Everyone in the region is so distrustful!" he said. "It is simply unreasonable. I am a respected man of the law from a distant land whose customs and attitudes are so different from those of Mortania." He paused a moment and then chuckled. "I am not offended, merely disappointed. No matter. I have made up my mind. I like you. I will dine with you tonight, at your home. No need to fuss about it. I will bring the feast and the entertainment."

Suddenly, little Wally, who had been sleeping soundly, began to cry. Aimas stood to check on him.

"Little one, you must be hungry!" Alicia said, as Aimas laid Wally in her arms. "Well, I suppose you don't need an introduction, sir, but this is my son . . ."

Alicia turned around to find Asmodeus quite gone.

2
A Most Generous Friend

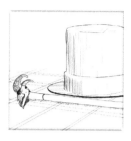

THE evening that Aimas and Alicia first hosted Asmodeus was the most memorable the couple had experienced in all their life. He spread a feast on their table like none other, with foods they had never seen let alone tasted. Everything was enticing. The fruits glowed in unimaginable color; the drinks fizzed and bubbled; the bread flaked and melted away in their mouths. Red, warm, and juicy, the roasted meat left them feeling powerful and a little dangerous. In fact, everything they ate made them feel different: bold, excited, exhilarated, overflowing with energy as if they could dance and dance and dance and never stop. And they could have, because Asmodeus also brought his players.

Dressed in sparkling gowns that bounced and swayed as they danced, women filled the air with high-pitched laughter. Fiddlers played so loudly and long that frayed horsehair flew about from the bow tips. The throng pounded the table and stomped on the floor until the clear, cold night gave way to the early morning fog.

It was only when the last player had finally left and the exhausted couple looked over the tipped chairs, littered table, and broken glass strewn across the sticky floor that they finally heard Wally's hoarse cry. He had been tucked away in his cradle, pushed into a corner and entirely forgotten. Alicia, horrified, picked up her little boy and kissed his flushed face over and over. She promised she would never be so cruel again.

Aimas was too tired to notice. He swooned as he made his way to the bed. His head ached. The last thing that interested him now was a cranky baby.

"And so the dream ends. Life was much more fun before Waljan came along," Aimas mumbled.

As the effects of Asmodeus's strange foods wore off, Alicia's frailty returned. Too tired to move, she lay in a corner of the devastated hut, holding Wally close. She vowed that if the opportunity arose again, he would enjoy the party from the comfort of his mother's arms.

The opportunity did arise again, and often. The couple hosted Asmodeus and his companions regularly. They saw very little of Asmodeus himself. He would come, lay out the feast, and get the party started. No one seemed to notice when he stepped away. He was certainly never the last to leave.

Alicia grew weaker. Recovering from her nights of fun took longer and longer. Yet the more they hosted Asmodeus's celebrations, the more Aimas wanted to celebrate, and the less he wanted to work. It became harder to feed and clothe the family, and he resented having to do so. They both realized that without Asmodeus's friendship they would have no food to eat at all.

One morning, Asmodeus dropped by unannounced, shortly before the sun had reached its peak. Aimas sat on his rotting porch stairs under the shade of a large walnut tree, whittling a stout chunk of wood. A lazy wind tossed the walnut's branches about, matching the aimless mood of the morning. Close by,

Waljan wriggled and cooed as his mother watched in a listless heap on the hammock.

"Is it a toy for little Wally, Aimas?" Asmodeus asked.

Aimas studied the stick and shrugged. "I don't know."

Alicia looked away.

"Hmm, well. At least you're making progress," Asmodeus cracked. "May I have a word?"

"As many as you like, my friend," Aimas replied.

"Lately you seem to have lost enthusiasm for your work. As fascinating as the scrap wood industry is, I thought you would be interested in a new opportunity."

Aimas dropped his stick. Standing, he straightened his greasy hair and tucked his crumpled nightshirt into his trousers. "Well, I would, my friend. I think I would. Doing what?"

"I need a problem solver. You have capable hands, a strong body. And I have a sense that you're good at solving problems. You see, from time to time I run into unreasonable people. People who don't see things the way I do. They cause trouble for me. I am a very busy man. I would simply need you to eliminate the problem. Do you see?"

"I think I do," Aimas said uneasily.

"Fine, fine. Excellent," Asmodeus replied.

"When do I start?" Aimas asked.

"After you have bathed, my dear Aimas, and burnt those rags you call clothing. I have brought you and your lovely wife a new wardrobe. We'll celebrate tonight, and tomorrow morning you will start your life anew!"

In the evening, dressed in their sumptuous new party clothes, Aimas and Alicia greeted Asmodeus and his entertainers. Over a crisp linen shirt, Aimas wore an embroidered silk vest with four ruby buttons running down the front. His wool pants were tucked neatly into high polished boots. Alicia's brightly colored embellished dress contrasted dramatically against her thin, paling complexion and hollowed eyes. It was as if the blood had run from her face, down her neck, and pooled in floral patterns all over her satin bodice. But with Asmodeus's party fare, the hypnotic music, and renewed hope for the couple's future, Alicia's youthful radiance returned. Once again, she was the beauty Aimas married. The couple agreed that Asmodeus was their most trusted and generous friend.

Starting the next morning and every day for weeks afterward, Aimas would leave home before sunup and return just in time to change for the night's festivities. One evening, Asmodeus threw open the front door of Aimas's hut in cheerful greeting. Poised to rush in, his players fell back. Aimas, stricken with concern, blocked their way.

"I am sorry, Asmodeus, but Alicia is too ill to celebrate today."

"Nothing to apologize for, dear Aimas. We can have jolly fun without her!" Asmodeus replied, pushing Aimas aside. Aimas shut the door against the players and faced a defiant Asmodeus.

"You don't understand, Asmodeus. She is very ill. I am worried about her."

"I understand perfectly, Aimas. Your wife is under a great deal of stress."

"I believe it's the festivities," the worried young husband confessed. "We do enjoy it, but it seems to cost us so much."

"The festivities? Nonsense," Asmodeus replied. "The revelry eases her hard work and brightens a life that would otherwise be dull and meaningless. You must know that. Have you not noticed how Alicia seems to come alive during our evenings together?"

"Yes, but overall, Alicia has gotten so much worse since we met you," Aimas replied.

The air in the room suddenly grew cold and heavy.

"Oh, I see. Blame me . . . blame your most trusted and generous friend. Honestly, Aimas. Alicia had taken ill long before I met you."

"Well, yes but . . ."

"Oh Aimas!" Asmodeus sneered. "Don't you see? It is so obvious. Who makes demands on your wife? You are gone all day. It can't be you. And I only give her what she needs." Asmodeus stared intently into Aimas's pained eyes. "It's the child. It's the child who sickened your wife, and it is the child who burdens her. He burdens you both. You know this. You've known it all along."

"But he's just a baby, Asmodeus . . ."

Asmodeus pressed Aimas into a corner like a cat toying with its prey. "You disappoint me, Aimas. I would have expected more gratitude from you. Are you willing to give up everything I have done for you? Think, Aimas. Wouldn't you rather laugh, dance, live, than plod along collecting sticks for a beggar's wage?"

"You know I would! But how can we blame Waljan for our situation?"

"So, you will blame me instead. You are fine with taking my money and leaving my friends waiting outside with the manners of a common peasant, but when I try to help you . . . to free you of the things in life that weigh you down, you turn on me. I don't need this. I am content to take my leave and find better friends."

"Please," said Aimas. "Don't be cross with us. We love your visits and your friends. We would be nowhere without you. I am just suggesting that we give Alicia time to rest."

"Yes, yes, of course," Asmodeus replied and turned away. "You say that now. Then it will be some other excuse and then another.

You are headed down a very bleak road, my friend. Assuming you ever really were my friend." At this, Asmodeus seemed suddenly lost and sad. His moods changed so quickly. It left Aimas confused and scrambling.

"What would you have me do?" asked Aimas.

Asmodeus challenged him, "Do you trust me?"

Aimas considered the question and slowly nodded his head.

"Then come away. You and Alicia come away with me. You have served me well these past few weeks, and I can use you in other areas. You can't imagine the things I can show you—things you've never seen. In my homeland there are cures that would permanently return Alicia to the healthy young woman you once knew. You can start a new life in a glorious land of wonders. But . . ." At this Asmodeus's flighty passion turned dark and sinister. "You must leave the child behind."

Aimas shook his head and turned away. "I can't, Asmodeus."

"It is for the child's own good, Aimas! Alicia cannot care for him; she is dying. And what can you do for him? He will be quite safe, I assure you. I know of a well-traveled place, sheltered from the rain and hidden from danger. Someone is bound to find him there and give him a good home."

Aimas faltered. Asmodeus could not be right. But Aimas found no error in his reasoning.

"You said you trusted me," Asmodeus prodded.

The sense of Asmodeus's argument and his concern for Alicia's well-being settled the matter. Whatever guilt Aimas felt for wanting to enjoy the pleasures of life at the expense of his son gave way to the hope that everyone would benefit from his decision. And so it was that Aimas and Alicia were long gone by the time Haden met little baby Waljan in the forest.

3
Give and Take

Bo Dog bounded from the porch to greet his masters as they cleared the stand of trees that lined the yard of their woodland home. The rustic mountain cabin perched in the center of the yard atop a slight grade. It was primitive but friendly, and well kept.

Wally tousled Bo's wiry coat and wrestled a bit before heading inside to wash up. "Sorry, pup, it's rabbit again tonight." The dog whined and frantically scratched his ear. "I know, I'm sick of rabbit, too."

"That dog is going to have to work for his rabbit one of these days, Boy," Haden said. "Now let's get inside. It's been a long day, and the sun is dropping fast. I'll grab some wood for the stove and be right behind."

"Yes, Sir." Although one would easily take them as family, Haden disapproved the title "father." They had settled on "Sir." Wally looked up to Haden as a good provider and hard worker. Haden was committed and dependable. And he had a certain affection for the boy. But he was more a steward than a father. He'd had no plans for family when he fell upon Wally in the Wood those many years before.

"Oh, and Waljan . . ."

"Yes, Sir?"

"I have something I need to run by you. Let's talk over dinner."

"Okay," Wally replied, unsure of the request. The two were together all day, every day. There was never a time they couldn't talk. Setting time aside seemed oddly formal. After a pause, Wally turned and darted up into the cabin, as if having answered his own unasked question.

Bo Dog stared at Haden, ears perked, eyes searching for a cue.

"What?" Haden snipped. But he couldn't resist that eager expression. "Come on, pooch, let's go get some wood for the fire." Haden lumbered over to the wood pile with Bo Dog wagging his heavy tail and snaking around Haden's heels. Haden grabbed an armful of split logs from the pile and made his way up the porch. But this time, Bo didn't follow. He stared into the woods, growling deeply. Haden surveyed the trees, graying in the waning light of dusk.

The orange glow of torchlight flickered between the pines and then broke through the brush. Bo threw off a sharp but happy bark, tumbling toward Penelope and her older brother, Culbert.

"Hey! Bo Dog! How've you been, pup?" Penelope said as the dog playfully pawed at her and rolled over in adoring submission.

Cullie took Haden's hand and shook it firmly. A young man of barely twenty years, he carried himself as one much older. He was tall and lanky with large owl-like eyes, a strong masculine jaw, and shapely lips.

"Culbert Longbow, what brings you here at this hour?"

"Well, Haden, Penelope told me about the stag, and I thought the least we could do is share some of the steaks from our kill.

And, apologize, of course. Isn't that right, Penelope?" Cullie shouted over Bo's boisterous yips and groans.

"Yeah," Penelope replied with flushed and newly cleaned cheeks. Her hair was brushed and plaited down her back, and she wore freshly laundered overalls. "Is Wally around, Mr. Haden?"

"Well, you're looking much more like the young lady I know than you did earlier today. Yes, he's here." Before Haden could direct Penelope to the cabin, Wally appeared at the door. Penelope ran up the stairs to greet him.

"It's late, Peep. What are you doing here?"

"You said I owed you a stag. The best I could do was a few steaks. It was Cullie's idea, actually." Penelope faltered a bit. "I'm . . . um . . . sorry about today, Wally . . . well, I'm not sorry I scared the stag, but I am sorry I ruined your hunt."

Wally wrinkled up his nose. "But . . . aren't they the same thing, Peep? That doesn't even make sense," Wally chuckled.

"Well, maybe not to you. But it should. Beautiful things should never have to die." Penelope said wistfully. The growing dark hid the tears that welled up in her eyes, but Wally could still hear them in her voice.

Wally shuffled his feet, hands pressed into his pockets, and looked around as if trying to find a mental escape route. "Well, you know you don't have to apologize to me, Peep. Besides, you're right," he conceded. "Beautiful things should never die." The lull returned until a chorus of tree frogs gave Wally a diversion. "Hey, we have polliwogs in the pond. With a torch, we could probably spot a few. Wanna take a look?"

Penelope perked up and called out to her brother, "Cullie, can I go look at the polliwogs with Wally?"

"Maybe next time. We have to head home," he replied.

"Why don't you stay?" Haden offered. "We haven't eaten yet, and those steaks look a lot more appealing than what we'd planned. Join us."

"We came on foot. It won't be safe to return if we wait much longer," Cullie explained.

"I'll take you back in the rig. It's fitting that we feast tonight, don't you think?"

Culbert agreed to stay, and the friends, now reconciled, ran for the trail head, torch in hand and Bo at their heels.

"Come on, Peep . . . I'll beat you there!" Wally challenged.

"But it's dark, Wally!" Penelope complained.

"Well then you better keep up since I have the torch!" Wally picked up his pace.

"Wally! That's not fair!"

"So now who's the baby, huh?" Wally laughed with playful vengeance, and the two disappeared down the path.

Haden yelled after them, "Don't be too long!" He and Culbert threw the steaks on a griddle and talked hunting, trapping, and the challenges of raising motherless children.

Wally and Penelope raced along the cool, powder-soft path. With Bo underfoot and an occasional tree root jutting up from the forest floor, it was a wonder they kept their feet in the twilight. But they were determined to make it a contest. The families of the Wood lived some distance apart, and Penelope was one of very few youngsters that Wally could call "friend." As she and Wally reached the little alcove where a pond formed each spring, the cacophony of frog song abruptly stopped. Bo ran to the water and sniffed around in the mud. Holding the torch out in front of him, Wally approached the pond and lit the surface. But the light couldn't penetrate the black mire in which the developing frogs hid.

"I could scoop them out for you," Wally said. "They just have their little stubby back legs. They wouldn't escape."

"I'm perfectly capable of catching polliwogs, Wally. Let's leave them alone. They're probably sleeping."

"You're a funny one, Peep. Do polliwogs even sleep?" Wally mused.

"Is there a place to sit?" Penelope asked. If we are really quiet, the frogs might start up again."

"Sure. I have a log over here." Wally took Penelope's hand and guided her over to the log. "A good time to start training Bo Dog for the field. Lie down, Bo, and be quiet." The three companions sat still for several minutes. A lone frog piped up. Another answered. And then, within seconds, the forest erupted in an amphibious symphony. Penelope smiled. That's better, Wally thought.

"It's been two years, Wally. I miss her every day."

"I know," Wally said.

"Sometimes I see her in my dreams. But each time, her face seems to fade just a bit more. And I realize that I am forgetting what my own mother looked like. It's like losing her all over again."

"Come over here, Peep." Wally took the torch and set it close to the water's surface. "Look in the water."

She did. "What am I looking for?"

"Your reflection."

Penelope questioned him silently and then stared at herself in the still, glassy pond.

"That's what your mom looked like." Wally handed Penelope

the torch and sat back down. "I'm jealous, you know. I miss my mother, too. And I never knew her. I don't have a face to forget. Even fading memories are memories, Peep. And if you forget them completely, those experiences still live inside you. They make you who you are."

Bo Dog jumped to his feet with a muffled woof!

"What is it, Bo?" Wally whispered. The dog began to growl menacingly. It was then that Wally realized how still and thoroughly black the night had become. A branch snapped in the distance. Bo exploded in a string of angry barks. He was still a puppy, but big enough to sound intimidating. A flurry of rustling and snapping came from the direction Bo faced, and then faded away into the distance.

"It's gone, but I think we'd better get moving, Peep. A single dying torch and an untrained pup make poor protection against a hungry predator . . . or worse."

"It's getting chilly anyway," Penelope said, trying to sound unconcerned. "And I am getting pretty hungry myself." She pulled up some withered sphagnum moss. "Here, this will help a little." Wrapping the moss tightly around the dying torch and blowing gently rekindled a bright blaze.

"Much better. Good thinking, Peep," Wally said as they walked on.

"Wally, what did you mean by 'or worse'? What could be worse than a hungry predator?"

"Oh. Well, a leshy, of course," Wally answered casually.

"You don't believe that stuff do you? Leshies are just folklore. Like flying horses and invisible castles. Grown-ups tell children that the leshy will steal them away if they wander off alone in the Wood. But I wander off all the time . . . "

"And have you ever noticed how nervous that makes Haden?" Wally laughed.

"Well, not once have I ever seen a giant shape-shifting creature," Penelope concluded. "I don't see why he should worry."

"Maybe you have seen one, you just don't know it." Wally teased. "Maybe it just looked like a tree, or a frog, or like me. Maybe I am leading you to your doom this very moment!"

Penelope giggled as Wally became more serious. "Some people think they are real. Sometimes things happen that can't be explained any other way. Haden once told me about a horse that had been eaten by something that left only the hooves behind. What animal does that?"

"If I were an animal in this forest, I would be more afraid of man than a fairy tale," Penelope suggested.

"In any case, Peep, one can't be too careful in the forest."

As Wally and Peep approached the last stand of forest trees, the savory mix of meat juices and wood smoke taunted them. Bo had already run ahead to beg for his portion. When they reached the trail head and started up the knoll toward the fire pit, they saw Cullie and Haden locked in a tense conversation above the sizzle of venison steaks.

"It's long overdue, Mr. Haden. You need to talk to him," Cullie implored. "Let us take the rig tonight. I'll bring it back by sunup."

"It's really not necessary," Haden insisted.

Being trackers and very aware of their physical surroundings, the men halted their conversation long before Wally and Penelope could make sense of it.

"What's going on?" Wally asked.

"You mean, what's coming off!" Haden said, turning

everyone's attention to food. "These steaks are just about ready. You two have excellent timing."

Wally thought venison had never tasted as good as it did that night. After supper, Cullie sang some old folk songs his dad had taught him when he was small, long before a tragic landslide robbed him and his sister of their parents. Wally knew some of the words, and they all joined in, including Bo Dog with his somber howl. Good friends, warm fires, starry skies, and rich food nourished Wally's spirit as well as his body. Here, at this moment, he was happy. Everything was just as it should be.

4
An Unexpected Storm

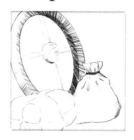

"BOY! I haven't got all day!" Haden bellowed from the top of his wagon.

"These pelts are heavy, Sir."

"Well, they don't get any lighter the longer you carry them," Haden said. "Let's go; I want to get to the Mercantile before that storm sets in. The wind is kicking up, and my old bones are feeling a change in the air."

"Yes, Sir," Wally replied dutifully and loaded the last bundle onto the cart. "What have you got here, Sir? This is the biggest load I've ever seen you carry."

"Well I . . . I have some extra business today," Haden replied. He settled into the seat and gathered the reins. "Let's get that load secured now."

Wally whistled for Bo as he tied off the last knot and scrambled up next to Haden. Bo Dog was out of sight. Wally couldn't even hear him scurrying around the yard. "Bo Dog! Let's go!"

"Bo's not coming with us, Wally. I don't need him getting into trouble in town."

"But where is he?" Wally asked, still scanning the yard. "I haven't seen him all morning."

"I let him stay with Cullie last night. Now sit down; we've got to get moving."

A snap of the reins set Maggie in motion with a shake of her black cropped mane. Their destination lay at the base of Castle Mount in a city of charming curiosities. Colors, textures, and noises filled the streets of Mortinburg. People bustled. Machines churned. Horse-drawn carts came and went. But whatever confident purpose or happy industry might be observed among the fray, there was always an insecurity, a tension like a drawn bow waiting to release its flaming arrow into the mist. No one really talked about it. Everyone felt it.

Legend held that a king surpassing all wisdom, beauty, power, and wealth once lived in a gleaming white castle that rose from the very center of the domain and cast light in all directions. So brilliant was the castle that it blended into daylight and became nearly invisible. Few Mortanians believed the castle existed. They explained that their mountain was named "Castle Mount" for its many sharp, spire-like peaks. Stories about the king were dismissed as fairy tales for children and comfort for the dying. But elders claimed that the castle, gleaming as bright as the sun, had stood on the mountain's peak since the beginning of time. Nothing is quite as invisible as something overlooked for its constant presence, nor as easily dismissed as the idle talk of old men.

When Wally was a young boy, Haden would tell him stories about the kingdom before bedtime. But he was too old for children's stories now. As the rig carried them out from the cover of tightly packed evergreens and onto the expanding plain, Wally took his turn at Maggie's reins. He eased against the backboard and stared across the grassy expanse as the leather straps bounced loosely from his light grip. The wagon tripped over the stony trail, jostling the two quiet figures side to side. Their silence made the call of a stray hawk all the lonelier.

"What's the matter, Waljan? You're awfully pensive today."

Wally shrugged.

"You know, when I was your age, I couldn't wait to get into all sorts of trouble in Mortinburg. But you brood all the way there. When we arrive, you sit inside the cart and drop below the planking or shadow me through the shops. You're strong for your age. You're healthy. You're going to be a man someday soon, and you can't go through life with your head down and your tail tucked under. What are you so afraid of?"

"I'm not afraid of anything!" Wally protested. "I just don't like Mortinburg. It's loud. It smells. It's crowded. And that old hag is always staring at me. I'd feel a lot better with Bo at my side."

Haden chuckled. "Afraid she's going to cast a spell on you?"

"It's not funny, Sir. There is something unsettling about her—about the whole place. It is not free and peaceful like Mortwood."

"Well, no, it's not like the Wood," Haden admitted. "But the underside of most things is dark and dirty, even Mortwood. Try looking from the top down. It's a nicer view."

As Wally pondered Haden's wisdom, the rig's spoked wheels creaked and moaned. Wally slapped Maggie's reins before an approaching hill. Haden sighed and then broke the awkward silence.

"You know, Wally, I am not very good at . . . I mean . . . I know you love the Wood. But living in the wilderness is not an easy life. It's not for everyone."

"We're not everyone, Sir."

"I know, but what I am trying to say is that I am not getting any younger."

"So, this is what you wanted to talk about last night? You don't need to worry about me, Sir. I'm getting taller and stronger. Soon I'll be old enough to care for both of us. I'm not going anywhere."

Haden smiled at Wally's dedication, but his heart sank at the hard realities that faced them.

The wind blew steady and cold when old Maggie pulled the cart up to the Mortinburg Mercantile. They had made good time. They could conduct their trades, load up new supplies, and be home by early evening. After the two unloaded, Haden went in to complete his business with the store owner, Josiah Constance, and Wally stayed with the cart. The boy had insisted that Maggie needed company, to which Haden had replied, "Of course."

Pressing his hands against the flatbed of the cart, Wally hopped up and sat. He ignored the throngs of carts, horses, and people passing this way and that. Women with baskets of goods and children in tow, gangs of young men searching the crowds for the prettiest faces and goading each other mischievously, a youngster herding geese with a stick: these were just the moving gears of civilized life.

Wally wrapped his arms across his chest to fend off the now biting wind and stared down at his dusty boots as he swung them slowly back and forth, back and forth. Suddenly, a flash of movement caught the corner of his eye. Oh, not again! Wally thought. A peasant woman, bedraggled and wide-eyed, ducked behind the side of the cart. Slowly, she raised her head, mumbling something Wally could not understand. Her yellowed smile revealed gaps where teeth used to be, and she let out a low, wispy chuckle like thorns rubbing against a window pane.

"Be gone, witch!" Wally yelled. He grabbed his cap and flapped it in her direction as if she were a stray dog. "Why do you keep hounding me?"

The hag had never done Wally any harm. But every trip into town he anticipated her unwanted leering. He was too unnerved to feel sorry for her, a discarded harlequin doll in faded rags that were once colorful and fancy.

As Haden took his leave of Mr. Constance, Wally moved to the front of the cart to check the horse's harness in preparation for the trip home. Haden lingered a moment, trying to find the right words. He couldn't avoid the subject any longer.

"Sir," Wally shouted over the noise of the busy street, "shouldn't we be headed back? The storm is on its way. We may not make it home in time."

"We are not going back home, Wally." Haden said.

"What do you mean we are not going home?" Wally objected.

Haden had already seen his best years when he first discovered Wally in the Wood, and he was weakening with age. Haden did not want to oblige Wally to nurse an old codger out in the Wood. So, he accepted Mr. Constance's offer of a small room in the Mercantile where he could be of use.

"The widow Pruitt has offered to give you a home, and teach you to read, write, and be a gentleman. You will have to work for your room and board, of course. But you're not afraid of hard work."

"I'm a woodsman, Sir! Waljan Woodland. I don't need letters and manners. I need the freedom of wilderness life. And I need to be with you."

"But Wally, she has two boys your age. You would have friends."

"I already have friends, Sir! I have Peep and Cullie. I don't need anyone else. I am not like the people here," Wally protested.

Haden sighed. "I know I should have told you sooner, Waljan.

I meant to. It just wouldn't come out, and then Cullie and Peep stopped by . . . I know you don't understand now, but this is a good situation for both of us."

"What about Bo Dog?"

"Mrs. Pruitt won't allow dogs. Penelope loves Bo as much as you do. He'll be happy with her."

"And who will I be happy with, Sir? You've thought of everyone's happiness but mine."

"No, Boy. This does not make me happy."

"Then let's go home, Haden. Please."

There was no use in Wally arguing. Haden's mind was made up.

5
On the Outside

"WALJAN!" screeched Mrs. Pruitt. "Waljan!" She never seemed to tire of his name. She screamed it hundreds of times each day followed by "fetch this," "fix that," "carry this," "be silent," or "stand still"! So often did Wally hear Mrs. Pruitt shout his name that he started to think maybe she had forgotten those of her own children.

Mrs. Pruitt wasn't a bad woman. She simply had an unfortunate combination of personal qualities that made her excessive in too many ways. And Wally didn't make it easy for her to see their arrangement as more of a benefit than a burden. He often daydreamed, never smiled, and rarely entertained a conversation. No one knew what his heart suffered. But it was obvious to everyone in the Pruitt household that their comfortably elegant home was the last place on earth he'd like to be.

"Waljan!" echoed down the hall, with Mrs. Pruitt right behind. She waddled around the corner, patting stray hairs back into her heavily teased up-do, and practically knocked Wally over. He had just finished rubbing a brilliant shine into her silver. "Oh, there you are! Can't you hear, Waljan? I am simply hoarse from calling you!"

That wouldn't be a bad thing, Wally thought.

"I was thinking, Waljan. I'd like to have Haden over for my next dinner party. The two of you can catch up on how you are settling in."

"Oh. Uh . . . He wouldn't come. Haden doesn't like being around a lot of people. He's used to being by himself."

"Well, how can you be so sure? You haven't seen him at all since you've arrived. I do think he would like to visit with you."

"I doubt that, Mrs. Pruitt. This was all his idea. I think he is happy with this arrangement."

"Well that's not a very good attitude, Walj—"

Wally interrupted her. "Excuse me, Mrs. Pruitt, but I think I should go check on the chickens. I heard some commotion out in the yard. You wouldn't want some critter getting into the coop." Then Wally abruptly left the room.

Despite Wally's refusal to see or speak to Haden, the separation pained him. He knew that Haden had made the best decision for both of them. Wally was just at the point where boys begin to show hints of manhood. Sometimes he felt like he could take care of himself, but deep down he knew that he needed looking after. He missed Haden's company and now, having another caretaker to compare with Haden, was certain his best childhood days were over.

Feeling guilty at his white lie, Wally decided he should check on the chickens even though he knew they were perfectly safe. He picked up an egg basket on his way out the back door and strolled over to the coop. As Wally gently coaxed the green, blue, and light brown eggs from underneath the hens, Caddock Pruitt and his twin brother, Tyre, came into the yard, kicking a leather ball back and forth.

"Hey, Wally, you in there?" they called.

Wally emerged with a full basket of eggs, blinking with the change of light.

"There you are. We need one more player to make a team. Have you ever played deflector ball?"

"I don't know what you mean," Wally answered. In the Wood, there were few open fields and even fewer youths for playing team games, even if the woodsmen had heard of "ball."

Bewildered, Caddock wondered, "What a rotten life you must have lived! What did you and your friends do in the forest for fun?"

"Caddock!" Tyre jabbed an elbow in his brother's side. "It's simple, Wally. One team tries to get the ball through the other team's goal. The deflector's job is to bat the ball away before it passes into the goal." Tyre dropped the ball at his feet with a heavy thud. "Here, stop this." Before Wally could anticipate what came next, the ball flew from the end of Tyre's foot like a comet toward Wally's head.

"What . . ." shot from Wally's mouth as he instinctively ducked. ". . . are you doing!" The ball smashed into the basket of eggs, catapulting them all over the yard and into the side of the coop. The chickens startled. Flapping and chattering, they escaped into the yard. Gooey yellow egg slime slid down the picket fence, pooled in the wheelbarrow, and coated the flower beds. Caddock and Tyre couldn't avoid laughing against their better judgment.

"You dolt!" Caddock teased. "You're supposed to hit it back!"

In the midst of the chaos, Mrs. Pruitt stormed through the back door. "What is going on here? Do you think we keep chickens for your recreation? Tyre! Caddock! Explain this mess."

"We were just kicking the ball around, Mother," Caddock replied, still giggling. "Waljan had the eggs . . ."

"Waljan!" Mrs. Pruitt interrupted, as she tended to do when she was in a hot temper. "I thought you came out here to quell some commotion, not to cause it!"

"But Mrs. Pruitt . . ." Wally implored.

"No 'buts.' If you think that I am going to put up with any of this behavior, you are dead wrong, young man. I would sooner throw you out on the street. I will not be taken advantage of. Do you understand me?"

"But, Mother . . ." Tyre said.

"Not another word!" Mrs. Pruitt demanded. "It is noble of you to protect Waljan, Tyre. But he needs to understand that this is not some wilderness cottage. It is a civilized home. Now you and Caddock go find amusement somewhere else. And you, Waljan Woodland, I want this mess cleaned up immediately." She retreated in a flurry and slammed the door behind her.

"Well, that didn't go so well, did it?" said Tyre. Caddock snickered despite his efforts to assume a more somber attitude. Wally glared back at them and began collecting broken shells.

"Sorry about that, Wally," Tyre said.

"Just go," Wally replied bitterly.

"Fine. So much for trying to be friends," Caddock quipped.

"If that's what you call friendship, I don't need it, thanks," Wally replied. "I have to get back to work."

"Let's go, Tyre. He would probably make us lose the game anyway. Let's go find someone who knows how to have fun." The boys ran off to meet their friends.

"I know how to have fun," Wally said to himself, staring at the eggy mess. "And this is not it." Wally started to regret his anger. A cooler head might have at least enlisted the boys' help in cleaning up. And it would have been much easier at the dinner table that evening if he'd had a couple of "comrades in arms" to help him stand against their mother's silent displeasure. "Settling in" felt more like hiking in wooden clogs than reclining in bedroom slippers.

Over the next few days, when Wally met Mrs. Pruitt for lessons, her haughty disapproval softened into a more businesslike attitude.

"These letters are the open-mouthed sounds, the vowels. Now, repeat after me, aaa-eh-ih-ah-uh."

Wally repeated, "Aaa-eh-ih-ah-uh."

"Something hurt, Wally?" Caddock's head popped around the corner. Tyre laughed from behind the wall.

"Boys, don't interrupt. And again, Wally, aaa-eh-ih-ah-uh."

Caddock strutted into the kitchen and grabbed two apples, tossing one to his brother, who seemed less interested in being a nuisance. Caddock leaned up against the kitchen sink and crunched hard into the apple, squirting the juice everywhere and chewing noisily.

"Really, Mrs. Pruitt, I think I have it . . ." Wally said.

"REPEAT! Aaa-eh-ih-ah-uh," Mrs. Pruitt insisted.

"Aaa-eh-ih-ah-uh."

Crunch! Caddock took another bite.

"Caddock! Tyre! Don't you two have something to do?" Mrs. Pruitt asked. "And again, Waljan, aaa-eh-ih-ah-uh!"

"Sure, Ma," Caddock responded. "But this is so interesting. I mean, Tyre and I were so little when you taught us to read, I don't remember having to cluck like a chicken. Aaa-eh-ih-ah-uh!"

Tyre covered his mouth and nose, chortling softly as Caddock kept up his comedy, "Are you sure it's going to work on wolf-boy here? I mean, he's almost full grown. You know what they say, you can't teach an old dog new tricks!"

Wally stared at the letters on the table, fuming.

"Oh, Caddock, stop being such a tease. Off with both of you. Wally and I have work to do. Now Wally, again, aaa-eh-ih-ah-uh."

Repainting the white picket fence followed Wally's humiliating lesson, and in the evening "wolf-boy" was forced to demonstrate for the family how he'd never been taught to set a formal table. *Let's see your pampered darlings build a fire, lay a trap, or skin a wildcat,* Wally argued in his head, the only place he allowed himself to.

After dinner, Wally retreated to his room. Although clean and comfortable, the room was still foreign to him, strange. A white eyelet spread covered the four poster bed, topped with pale, pink pillows; and a small painting of goldfinches hung askew on the opposite wall.

Wally looked out the open window, beyond the shake rooftops toward the Mercantile, where Haden now lived. The lacy sheers flitted in the cool breeze. He recalled the songs that Peep and Cullie would be singing about this time of night. Every evening the Longbows sang songs in tribute to their parents. They were probably doing that right now, with Bo Dog howling at their feet. Wally hoped they were missing him too. Fighting back hot tears of acute loneliness, he wished he could fly home to the Wood or free himself from the resentment and anger that separated him from Haden.

On the desk below the window, Mrs. Pruitt stored a little letter box filled with paper, an ink well, and little nibbed pens.

Wally might have written Haden a letter if he knew how. After this morning's lesson he wasn't sure learning to read and write was worth the trouble. Wally stood gazing out the window at the lanterns lining the streets of Mortinburg. A steadier wind kicked up. Rain was on its way.

In his reflective state, Wally realized that in the many weeks he'd been in Mortinburg, he had never really explored his room. He was here so seldom, really only to sleep. But the week's events ate at him. He knew sleep would come slowly or not at all, so he sat down at the desk before him and scooted in. The little cane-backed maple chair groaned at the joints.

As he pulled open a little drawer in the front of the desk, odds and ends slid forward and came to a halt against the front board. Nibs. A small pile of tissues. A tattered card with the letters J and A and a skull embossed in gold. A ball of thread with a needle tucked through. A little book. Then, something unusual caught his eye.

Wally picked up a round object obscured by dust and what looked like tree sap or brown shoe polish. The dust wiped away easily enough, revealing a smooth gem-like surface, but the brown substance was hard and tacky. The object was heavy, as any rock its size would be, but unusually warm. He rolled it around in his hands and watched the light bounce off the cleaner parts.

Wally shuddered with the increasing chill pouring in. He set the rock down and reached for the window pane. A raindrop hit his cheek. Then another. Before he pulled the pane closed, a voice cried, "Come back to me!"

The voice was so faint that Wally wasn't sure if he'd imagined it. He spun around. No one had entered the room. Curious, he scanned the street below. But the only figures he could make out were the trees that lined the street, their massive, tangled heads swaying with the wind. The flickering lamplight just made the dark corners even darker on this moonless evening.

The sky flashed. Wally felt a pang of sympathy for whoever was out there, about to get drenched. In seconds, the drips became drops and the drops, became a steady rain. Wally shut the window and drew a set of heavy drapes against the lightening. Yawning, he settled into bed. As soon as he pulled up the covers, he heard it again from the window.

"Come back to me!"

Wally focused on the stone, still resting on the desk where he'd left it. Slowly, he pulled the covers aside and eased himself out of bed. Wally picked up the stone and brought it to his ear. Nothing.

Feeling a little foolish, he said at last, "Oh, Wally, you must be more tired than you thought!"

He dropped the stone back in the drawer and slipped back into bed.

6
A Truce

"COME back to me!" Penelope screamed as the rain came pouring down. Wally cried, "Peep!" as Bo Dog barked and snapped ferociously at his side. Mrs. Pruitt grabbed Penelope and carried her off, chanting, "No dogs allowed! No dogs allowed! No dogs allowed!" Thunder cracked.

Wally jolted awake to the sound of Tyre and Caddock drumming the wooden desk with their fists and laughing.

"So, what's a 'peep,' Wally?" Caddock asked in hysterics.

"Whadya doin'?" Wally slurred groggily. "Gid outta here!"

"Not without you, Sleeping Beauty," said Tyre. "We are on strict orders from Ma to get you out of bed."

Tyre threw open the drapes. Sunbeams shot through the window and directly into Wally's eyes. He recoiled and sheltered his face.

"Get out!" he yelled. "I'll be down in a minute. But not until you leave!"

The twins snickered and left Wally exhausted, disoriented, and angry. He plopped back onto his pillow and tried to figure out what day it was. Then he recalled his dream. *Penelope? No dogs allowed?* Wally tossed his bed sheets aside and dragged himself out of bed. With eyes still swollen and half-closed, he staggered his way to the water bowl. Instinctively, he scooped his hands into the bowl and splashed his face. By the time he realized that the Pruitt boys had recently filled the bowl with freshly whipped shaving cream, it was already covering his hands and spread across his face. He groped for the towel that the boys had taken away as the final touch to their nasty prank and, not finding it, used his bedclothes instead.

By the time Wally finally got to the breakfast table, clean, dressed, and alert, Mrs. Pruitt was incensed.

"I am sorry, Waljan," she said coolly. "But breakfast was served an hour ago."

Wally kept the shaving cream prank to himself and quietly suffered the consequences of his late start. He had been in the house long enough to know that Mrs. Pruitt would side with her twin sons in any conflict.

"Now, you have completely disrupted my day. I am going to need you to run into town and pick up some things at the Mercantile," Mrs. Pruitt continued.

"Alone?" Wally asked, meekly.

"Is there any reason a boy your age cannot run a simple errand unattended? How on earth did you survive in the wilds of Mortwood?" Mrs. Pruitt prodded.

"No . . . it's not that, ma'am. It's just the hag . . . there's this old . . ."

"What on earth are you babbling about, Waljan? I have no time for nonsense. If I go into the Mercantile myself, I may lose my composure and give Haden a piece of my mind concerning your arrangement here. Now, if you value having a place to stay, you will do what I say."

"Yes, ma'am."

Until he was out in the sunshine, Wally didn't realize how much he needed to be away from the Pruitts that morning. Walking through the residential areas of Mortinburg, he noticed how different it was from downtown. Just beyond the cobblestone walkways, large trees overrun by songbirds guarded the tidy little cottages that lined the street. Informal gardens perfumed the summer air, and the laughter of young children echoed from a distance. The closer he got to the center of town, the more uplifted Wally felt, despite his grumbling stomach. He slowed his pace to make the errand last as long as possible, greeting people politely on the way and taking in the sights and sounds of city life.

Turning a corner and passing the courtyard, Wally noted the time on the Mortinburg clock tower. Ten-fifteen. He passed a street that ended at a large mansion with a carved colonnade, black shutters, and a large red door. He walked by the herbalist's shop, the farmer's market, and the smithy, all busy with customers.

But the next building, which housed the Sweets Shop just the day before, was abandoned. The front of the shop was blackened with soot, and the windows were smashed. Inside, jars of confections covered the floor, dissolving into a kaleidoscopic pool. The entrance to the store was roped off, and a few people peered in from the street-talking to each other in hushed voices. Wally's curiosity needled him, but he continued on his errand.

Finally, Wally reached the Mercantile's wooden promenade, under which the hag typically hid. He stopped. The distance between where he now stood and the Mercantile's entrance at the center of the walkway seemed the longest stretch of his journey. He looked for signs of his stalker. A bit of movement and a puff of dust glided out from under the stairs. She was there.

Wally waited for the right moment. A group of women, engrossed in conversation, didn't even notice Wally strategically squeeze himself among them. Unaware, they escorted him right through the front door. Wally broke away from the women and into the middle of a heated discussion, huddled around Mr. Constance.

"I'm telling you, he has no right! No right at all! Where in our charter do we allow for the city to employ a gang of henchmen to harass our neighbors?" one man asked.

"Other towns in Mortania have a police force. Why shouldn't we?" argued another.

A middle-aged woman countered, "They are not police; they are goons!"

Haden had just entered and settled back against a wall of feed sacks, arms crossed and head bowed. Mr. Constance leaned into the counter, his hands flat against the surface as if bracing himself against his own anger.

"No, Madam," he thundered. "The goons are those who set fire to the Sweets Shop last night. They are the types who pick my locks in the middle of the night and help themselves to drinks and free equipment. They take to the streets harassing people and scaring the horses. These things are happening more and more, and we need help from our city officials. Look, I don't see what harm can come from the judge delegating law enforcement responsibilities. The town is getting too big and too busy for us to think of ourselves as a small, tight-knit band of neighbors any more. Haden and I are vulnerable here at the store. We live here!"

At the sound of his name, Haden looked up and then noticed Wally in the background. He saw his opportunity to break away from the argument. "Well, Waljan! Can I help you with something? Excuse me, folks. I had better help the customers." Haden approached Wally and was met by downcast eyes and a stony expression. Wally abruptly thrust a supplies list at Haden. "Oh. That's how it is, huh? I see," said Haden, playing along. "Okay, sir, let's take a look. Beets, whitewash, bar soap, half-inch rope . . . hmm. Would that be hemp, jute, or cotton fiber rope, sir?"

Wally looked up. "What?"

"Hemp, jute, or cotton fiber?"

"Well, I didn't ask. You always used to get hemp rope, so I just assumed . . ." Wally's voice trailed off and he dropped his gaze.

"Wally. You don't look well."

"Sir?"

"Your lips are white, and you have bags under your eyes big enough to store a wagon load."

"Oh. Well, I didn't sleep too well last night, and I haven't had any breakfast."

"No breakfast? That woman is supposed to be feeding you!" Haden said angrily.

"It's my fault. I slept in. Anyway, I need that stuff if you don't mind. She asked that you put it on account."

"First things first. You get your tail into that back room and sit at the kitchen table. I'm going to get you something to eat, and then, while I get these items together, you are going to lay down on that cot and rest. I am not letting you leave with this order otherwise. Got that?"

Wally nodded, betraying relief, and started toward the back room, but stopped. "What about the rope?"

"Oh. Mrs. Pruitt always gets cotton rope. She's allergic to hemp and jute. Breaks out in a horrible oozing rash. It's not pretty."

Wally protested, "Well then, why did you ask?"

"I just wanted to get you to look me in the eye."

Wally rolled his eyes at Haden's clever ruse and disappeared behind the curtain that separated the store from Haden's living quarters.

About an hour later, Haden roused Wally with warm soup, a seed cake, and fresh berry pie. As Wally dug in, he could feel his energy rushing back.

Haden sat with Wally as he ate. "I made the pie myself. Josiah has some early fruiting vines in the back."

Haden's concern and generosity made it nearly impossible for Wally to hold on to his resentment. But he still felt that his situation was unfair.

"I had no illusion that this change would be an easy one, Wally." Haden admitted. "We are not always in control of our circumstances, but we still must make the best of them. Do you think I was out hunting for a son to raise when I stumbled over you in the Wood? I didn't know how to hold you, to feed you, burp you, wash you. I had nothing to wrap you in; didn't know what it meant when you cried or drooled or threw up. For the first year, I was sure I was going to drop you on your head! But I had two choices: I could leave you to die in the Wood, or I could learn how to care for a baby. And that was not really much of a choice. Now, it's your turn to learn something new."

"Haden, if I could just go visit Peep and Cullie. And Bo. If I could just see my friends from time to time," said Wally.

"It's a long trip, Wally. One that I am having a hard time making anymore." Haden's heart ached seeing the loneliness in Wally's eyes. "All right. Every few months at most."

"Really? How soon can we make our first trip?"

"Well, we are expecting a wagon from the Wood tomorrow.

I will send word back to Cullie, and then we'll have to wait for a response. It's going to be at least a couple weeks before we can know."

"Oh, that's great! Thank you, Sir!" Wally nearly knocked Haden over with an enthusiastic embrace.

"Whoa, now!" said Haden, laughing. "Okay, enough of that. Now, before I forget, would you do Josiah a favor on your way home? A customer left a box on the counter. I need you drop it off. I put it in with Mrs. Pruitt's order."

"Sure. Where?"

"There is a street down past what's left of the Sweets Shop that leads straight to it, the mansion with the big white columns," Haden replied.

"Yes, I passed it on the way here," said Wally. "I saw what happened to the Sweets Shop. Is that what everyone was arguing with Mr. Constance about?"

"Seems so. I walked in just before you did. Everyone has an opinion about how to address the crime problem. When people live so close together, there is a lot more to work out between folks. It's not like in the Wood where you just mind yourself."

Wally smiled at Haden's mentioning the Wood. "I'd better go. I've been here too long already." He ran out of the living quarters and picked up the crate of supplies. It was a little awkward, but light enough. Cautiously, he approached the door of the Mercantile and listened for the hag's raspy mouthbreathing. She would never come into the store but would often park by the door and peer in, sometimes earning a bit of food or a warm cup of coffee.

The way seemed clear. Wally imagined that the hag was looking for someone to curse and that he must avoid her spells at all cost. Perhaps he was too old for such games, but it was an entertaining diversion. Wally readied himself for a sprint. "One, two, three . . . go," he whispered and bolted out the door, thundering down the wooden promenade. He leapt off the walkway to the unpaved road, stirring up a dust cloud behind him. Dashing through the city streets, Wally passed the post office, Matterson's Eatery, Sandy's Saddle Shop, and the Inn. He didn't slow down until arriving safely back at the Pruitt home.

7
Secrets of the Heart

WALLY kicked open the Pruitts' gate and gleefully jogged up the back walkway. Memories of the Wood possessed him. All he could think of on his way back from town was Peep, Cullie, and Bo Dog, and the chance to shoot his bow once again. He recalled the pine-scented air and the delicate wild flowers, riding Maggie through the trails, and fishing the stream off Promise Rock.

He leapt over a mud puddle that had curiously appeared since the morning and then bounded up the porch stairs, two steps at a time. When his foot hit the porch landing, it slipped on a large slick of mud waiting above the last stair. Wally tried in vain to regain his footing, scrambling jig-like and spreading the ooze everywhere. He tumbled down the stairs and landed in the mud puddle, followed by the box of supplies. Dazed, he lay there a moment, muck seeping through his clothes. He waited for the twins to appear. No one came snickering around a corner, no snide comments from a safe distance.

Wally lifted himself slowly. After wiping his muddy hands on his trousers, he began picking up the contents of Mrs. Pruitt's order: soap, hair clips . . . a box? Mrs. Pruitt hadn't ordered a box. He examined the red mahogany lid embossed with a golden goat skull. Then he made the connection. He had been so enthralled with the idea of visiting Peep that he had completely forgotten to make the delivery Haden had asked! Wally looked around, hoping that no one else saw his embarrassing ordeal. All was quiet. His curiosity took hold, and he peered into the mahogany box. No harm could come from just looking.

A brilliant ruby heart, as big as a walnut, glinted in the sunlight. It was the most beautiful thing Wally had ever seen. Under it lay a folded slip of paper. Wally couldn't resist. He pulled it out and tried his hardest to string the letter sounds together. It was useless. He did, however, make out the signature as it was two letters he'd seen before, "J. A."

All of a sudden, a melancholy overtook Wally. He thought of home, and a keen sense of loss overwhelmed him. The sadness of never having known his mother and father, the frustration of his current situation, the separation from those he loved, all of it came flooding over him at once.

"Waljan!" cried Mrs. Pruitt from inside the house. "Waljan, are you back yet?"

Wally tucked the note back underneath the gem, slammed the box closed, and hid it in his pocket. Something told him that the box was a very personal and private affair. He didn't want to be responsible for Mrs. Pruitt finding the note and spreading whatever sentiments it might contain.

Hastily, Wally wiped his eyes, cleared his throat, and called back, "Yes, ma'am!" Then, he picked up the crate and carefully climbed the stairs, avoiding the booby-trap. "The Mercantile was really busy today. I had to wait."

"That was some wait, Waljan. You've been gone hours," Mrs. Pruitt complained from inside the house.

"Well, it didn't help that I took a spill off the back porch."

Mrs. Pruitt came to the porch door. "Oh, dear, Waljan! Look at you! Did you get hurt? That was very clumsy of you."

"I'm okay, but there is mud all over the porch. I should go clean it off before someone does get hurt," Wally explained.

"Oh . . . how strange. I wonder if the boys know anything about that." Mrs. Pruitt blushed a bit. "Well, that is surprisingly thoughtful of you to take care of it." She took the crate from Wally and started to unpack her order. "Considering the lateness of the day, why don't you take the rest of it off? After you clean the porch, of course."

"Thank you, ma'am!" Wally replied, relieved that he would have time to deliver the box for Haden after all.

Dutifully, Wally washed down the porch. Then, he changed his clothes and made his way back into town. In strange contrast to his lighthearted trip home, Wally's return to town exhausted him. The joy of visiting Mortwood that possessed him earlier was replaced by the overwhelming sadness of not being there now. He dragged his feet, stopped often, and lost sight of his purpose more than once.

A group of boys, led by Caddock and Tyre Pruitt, caught up to Wally from behind and surrounded him like gnats.

"Hey, wolf-boy!" Caddock said. "Where are you off to?"

Wally ignored him and picked up his pace. The gang followed. One of the others taunted him. "Cat got your tongue, orphan?"

"Maybe he bit it off when he fell in the mud, boys!" The group broke out in cruel laughter and jesting. "Too bad we weren't there to see it!"

"Lay off, guys!" Tyre finally said. Then, toughening, he added, "You're just wasting your time."

Wally and the swarm arrived at the street that led to the house with white columns. Wally turned and shot a menacing glance at each of the boys. But he said nothing. Caddock noticed the box Wally clutched protectively at his side.

"Whatcha got there, lodger?" Caddock said.

Wally turned down the side street toward the mansion, marching with renewed purpose. Caddock followed close behind, but his entourage held back.

"Hey, I'm talking to you, wolf-boy!" Caddock grabbed Wally's arm and swung him around and then reached for the mahogany box. But Wally would not let go. For a split second the boys were locked together.

Caddock was instantly assaulted with feelings of inadequacy and failure. He felt exposed, foolish, irrelevant, and discarded. He turned around to see his gang watching from half a block away and immediately let go of the box.

"Hey! Where are you guys going?" he demanded angrily.

"Come on, Caddock," Tyre yelled back. "Let's go play ball."

Caddock turned back to Wally. "Catch you later, loser," he quipped and ran off to meet up with the gang.

Wally continued on. As he approached the iron gate, it seemed to grow in all directions until it stood before him like a massive sentry bellowing, "No passage here!" He pulled the latch, and the gate screamed opened, nonetheless. Inside the spacious yard, he felt very small. He followed the walkway to a wide staircase that led up through the columns to the door. In the center of the door hung an ornate brass knocker shaped like a goat skull. Its beauty struck Wally. He'd never considered the skull of any animal to be decorative. A brass plate positioned just below the skull had a J and an A engraved on it.

He pulled out the old tattered card that he had retrieved from his desk drawer before leaving the house and compared it. They were the same. Wally reached up and lifted the skull knocker away from its base. When released, the knocker fell hard against the door and sent a hollow, booming echo throughout the house. A servant opened the door, followed by the homeowner himself, dressed in a housecoat and elegant leather slippers.

"Thank you, Baxter, you may go," the homeowner said.

"I have a delivery from the Mercantile, sir," Wally said, holding out the mahogany box. His voice quavered, and his throat tightened up.

"Excellent! It has been found. Thank you," said the man. He took hold of the box, but Wally's grip tightened. The man studied Wally's expression closely and then jerked the box away. "Something torments you," the man said with an unsettling grin. "You're Waljan. The orphan that Josephine Pruitt took in, no?"

"Yes, sir," Wally replied somberly.

"Yes. Well, thank you. Good day." The man shut the door abruptly, and Wally was left staring up at the door knocker.

As if just awoken from a dream, he felt disoriented. He turned and looked toward town, then back toward the Pruitt's. Now what, he thought. With the rest of the afternoon to himself, he had no idea how to fill his time.

Steadily, as he descended the porch stairs and made his way to the front gate, his head cleared. It occurred to him how strange his exchange with the stranger was. He hadn't even introduced himself. Wally realized that he was just a delivery boy. There was no reason for the man to be polite. It was just that people usually were in that situation.

Thirsty, Wally decided to venture into town for a drink and

then explore the surrounding wilderness. One didn't have to travel too far out of the city limits to forget civilization for an afternoon. He stopped in at Geezer's Geysers, a little restaurant and bar that hosted evenings of entertainment for hard working Mortinburgans. At this hour, though, Geezer's was quiet with an occasional patron grabbing a quick lunch.

Mingled with the aroma of old wood, the acrid scents of yeasty beer and last night's tobacco greeted Wally as he passed through the heavy oak door. The restaurant was dark but not gloomy. Wally approached the counter and hopped up on one of the wooden bar stools.

"Well, there, young man," the proprietor said, "What can I get for you?" He was a hunched old man with smiling eyes and a downy white mustache that hung below either side of his chin. His bent posture made him smaller than he should have been, judging from his large, gnarled hands.

"Well, sir, I don't have any money. But I was hoping you could spare a glass of water, Wally answered.

"Hmm. Well, I don't know. Have any gold in them teeth?" the man asked, squinting one eye and flashing a sideways smile.

Wally just stared.

"Oh, my, we are serious today, aren't we!" the man said, chuckling. "Water it is."

Wally pulled out the card again and studied the letters. They just looked like strings of sticks and noodles. He turned the card around and around in his fingers as he watched the old man grab a glass from the shelf and dust it with a white rag. As the man twisted the white rag around the inside of the glass, Wally noticed a spherical object tucked just under it, pressed into the palm of his hand. As if without thinking, the man tossed the rag to the side, set the object by the sink, and opened an ice box. The object looked exactly like the sap-covered stone that he'd found in his room at Mrs. Pruitt's, but cleaner. The man turned to speak but paled upon seeing Wally's eyes fixed on the stone. He quickly grabbed the object and dropped it into his pants pocket.

"So, my dear penniless patron, did you want a slice of lemon with your water?"

"Oh, you don't need to go to any trouble," Wally said.

"No trouble at all. I don't like trouble," said the bartender mysteriously, as he plopped a slice of lemon and three cubes of ice into Wally's glass.

Although he had a sense that the question would not be welcomed, Wally mustered the courage to ask, "Sir, if you don't mind my asking, what was that thing you put in your pocket?"

The man searched Wally's eyes and set the glass before him. "Nonpaying customers get water. Maybe even a slice of lemon if they are lucky. But they don't get to ask personal questions." Then he smiled with a jaunty air. "I don't think I've seen you around here before."

"I'm Waljan Woodland, sir. I am a friend of Haden Hunter and Josiah Constance."

"Oh yes! You're the one who lives with Josephine Pruitt just outside town. Wow, that must be quite a row to hoe!"

"It can be, sir," Wally admitted.

"My name is Gerald Guest, but everyone calls me Geezer, or Geez for short." The man winked playfully at Wally. He glanced over at the calling card that Wally had dropped on the counter, his smile fading. "So, you his friend, too?"

"I'm sorry . . . whose friend?" Wally asked.

"Well, the judge's of course. You got his calling card there."

"Oh! Is that what this is? Mrs. Pruitt is teaching me to read. Well, trying to anyway. I was just by his house making a delivery from the Mercantile. He didn't introduce himself when he answered the door. Do you know the judge?"

"Off-limits, son. That's a personal question," Geez objected.

"Okay, but you asked me the same question. And I answered you. I guess that means I can upgrade my water to a soda?"

Geez relaxed and nodded. "You win." He grabbed a chilled bottle from the ice box, popped off the cap, and set it before Wally. "Your soda, sir." Then his voice dropped. "Everyone knows the judge. But don't mistake that to mean that everyone likes the judge. In fact, if I were you, I would stay as far away from that man as possible, you understand? But you didn't hear that from me."

8
An Overzealous Fire

FOR the next few weeks, Wally managed to keep his spirits high. Word came from Mortwood that Cullie and Peep were leaving the Wood for a month to help a distant cousin plant his winter crops. They hoped Wally and Haden would visit when the Longbows returned. The delay disappointed Wally at first. But the anticipation of escaping to Mortwood at all made everything in Mortinburg more tolerable, even the twins' trickery.

They started as childish pranks, a way to get Wally's attention. But over time, the twins' antics grew more elaborate and hostile. Caddock and Tyre soon learned, however, that Wally's tolerance had limits. After one particular and difficult day that ended with scrubbing Mrs. Pruitt's slab floor, Wally straightened his aching back and stretched his sore muscles. Mrs. Pruitt had planned an elegant party for that evening, and Wally knew she would be pickier about his effort than she would be about her own.

An important man from town had been meeting with Mrs. Pruitt frequently. That night she planned to introduce him to her family and friends. Mrs. Pruitt had been widowed at a young age and was lonely for companionship. As a middle-aged woman, she was heavy-set, but still lovely. Although Wally more often saw her scowl, her occasional smile was rather endearing, and Wally believed that she must have been stunning in her youth. Entertaining regularly, Mrs. Pruitt hoped that her hospitality would lure an eligible bachelor. The word in town was that it had.

Satisfied that he had done his best, Wally collected the wire hair brushes, the dripping rags, and the pail of dingy water and headed out to the side yard. Upon his return several minutes later, he pushed through the door. A jolt to the head knocked Wally to the floor with a "Thwang!" and a "Splursh!" Wally couldn't see, and in his confusion he frantically tried to pick himself up. Instead, he slid around in a warm velvety slime.

The sharp, sweet stench of rancid bacon surrounded him. Explosive laughter, followed by the thundering of running feet, faded away down the hall. When Wally finally steadied himself and removed the pail that had landed over his head, he met a dreadful sight. The floor, walls, ceiling and door were splattered with globs of dripping goo. The pail in which Mrs. Pruitt stored her months' worth of bacon had been balanced on the top edge of the side door waiting for a victim. From his toes a violent roar escaped him, "When I get ahold of you . . ."

Wally's anger was answered with a fearful reply, "Who is that shouting? What is going on? Waljan!" Mrs. Pruitt was making her way to the kitchen. She would not find him there.

* * * * *

When Haden opened his door to frantic pounding, he expected to find a disgruntled Mrs. Pruitt. He did not expect a throng of supporters lined up behind her.

"What is all this, now?" Haden asked. "Have we declared war, my friends?"

"You know full well why we are here, Haden. My friends and I should be enjoying a night of fine dining and socializing. Instead, it has been ruined and we are forced to confront you over this wretched business! Where is that feral child you brought into Mortinburg?" Mrs. Pruitt demanded.

"Well, Mrs. Pruitt, since you agreed to care for the boy, I might ask you the same thing," Haden replied.

"Are you telling me he's not here?" Mrs. Pruitt pressed.

A tall, elegant man, overly dressed for this occasion, stepped forward. Leaning on a black walking stick and sniffing deeply he said, "Mmmmm . . .I smell . . .bacon." He looked knowingly at Mrs. Pruitt.

"I'm sorry, I don't think we've met," Haden said to the man.

Gasps and chuckles resounded through the party.

"Why, you are the new store hand, aren't you? You must have seen me come into the Mercantile on occasion," the man answered.

"A lot of people come into the store, sir," Haden said.

"But few hold a high position in town. I am Mortinburg's chief justice, Judge Asmodeus, at your service." He handed Haden a calling card.

"At Mrs. Pruitt's service," Haden insisted. "Well, your honor, I am guilty as charged. You do smell bacon. I have spent most of my life hunting wild boar, and I must confess to enjoying a little bacon from time to time."

Haden looked away from the judge's uncomfortable glare and addressed the crowd, "Now look, I don't know what this is all about. But people know me as a man of my word. Of all the people in this town, I would be Wally's first refuge in times of trouble. I assure you he will turn up, and we will get this all straightened out, whatever it is. But not now. It's late. And we shouldn't be making such a ruckus while people are trying to settle in for the evening. Good night."

Haden shut the door on Mrs. Pruitt's last "But . . ." and tended the overzealous fire that crackled and smoked on the hearth, fueled by Wally's greasy clothes. He fetched an extra bar of soap from the Mercantile's shelves and headed into a back room where Wally sat like a dejected river rat in a tub of steaming water.

"Well, your trousers made an outstanding fire, Waljan. It's making me hungry," Haden joked.

"It's not funny, Sir," Wally sulked. "Was that Mrs. Pruitt?"

"Yes," Haden sighed. "And she brought half of Mortinburg with her. You must have made quite a mess over there." Wally stayed silent, poking at the silky soap bubbles that surrounded him. "Still," Haden continued thoughtfully, "it doesn't make sense. They can't have come all the way to town over spilled bacon fat. It's a bit overblown."

"Why did you send me over there in the first place?" Wally complained. "She is not going to forgive this and none of it was my fault. I did my best, and those twins . . . they hate me, Sir. They hate me for no reason. I just want to go home."

"Mortinburg is home, Wally. And they don't hate you. They're just not used to having you around the house yet. They'll warm up to you, eventually. You'll see. You'll become friends in time," Haden said.

"No, we won't because I am not going back," Wally stated firmly.

"Oh yes, you are going back, and just as soon as the sun creeps through that window tomorrow morning. It took a lot of convincing for Mrs. Pruitt to take you in. Now, I know it's hard. She isn't the kindest woman, but you haven't exactly been warm and chummy. You are too quick to punish and too slow to forgive. Wally, you have got to recognize the good that people do for you. Things could be a lot worse."

Wally disagreed, but he knew it would not do to argue with Haden. Instead, he retreated into his own thoughts. Finally clean and dreadfully sleepy, he lay on a bed of flour sacks that Haden arranged for him by the fireplace. The flames danced his glassy eyes to sleep.

When Wally awoke, the moon was still high, lighting the street in front of the Mercantile. Unfortunately, the awning that covered the promenade blocked any light from entering the store windows. Wally didn't dare wake Haden or Mr. Constance by using a lamp. Instead, he groped around in the dark.

Wally had all the supplies anyone would need to survive in the wild right there in the store, if only he could distinguish a case of matches from a set of playing cards, or a can of soup from a can of paint. Keenly aware of the time he was wasting, Wally reasoned that finding clothes was top priority. He could forage for food and start fires by hand if he must.

A cleverly knotted blanket doubled as a sack. In it, Wally wrapped some essentials found by chance while searching for suitable clothes: a knife, some rope, a handful of beef jerky, and a small bottle of all-purpose elixir that was known to battle insect bites and infections. He rolled up a random pair of trousers, hoping for the best, and tucked them into the blanket sack. Finally, he pulled a cowhide jacket over his nightshirt and slipped out the back door.

In the morning, it was Mrs. Pruitt who answered the door to a pounding that echoed through her large home. Haden was furious that he had entrusted Wally's care to Mrs. Pruitt, only to have the boy run away.

"What do you mean he's gone?" Mrs. Pruitt asked.

"I mean he's gone. He stayed the night at the Mercantile, and, when I got up this morning, he was gone."

"The judge warned me about this, about taking an orphan in. He said they were unstable."

"And what does the judge know about it? I have raised this boy from infancy!" Haden said.

"Well, I am sure you did your best being an old bachelor . . ."

"Yet despite my limitations I have never had a problem with Waljan. Sure, he complained a bit. But he worked hard and never caused trouble. He certainly wouldn't intentionally spoil your dinner party. Those little pranksters of yours have made his short time here miserable, and now who knows what will happen to him? If he is injured, Madam, it will be on your head, and I will hold you responsible."

Mrs. Pruitt felt a pang of guilt. "Well, I suppose the twins have been a little too rough. If you find the boy, we can give him a second chance."

"If I find him, Mrs. Pruitt, I may give you a second chance," Haden replied and left in search of Wally.

9
The Wall

IT is one thing to want to leave a place behind and quite another to have a place to go. Wally wasn't even sure another place existed. Mortwood and Mortinburg were the only places he knew. He could return to his forest home and wait for Peep and Cullie to return from the farm. But only the most skilled woodsmen traveled Mortwood alone. Besides, Haden would find him there. Wally didn't want to be found. He'd been given up twice. Now it was time for him to try life on his own terms.

So, Wally made his first truly independent decision. He chose an untried path. He would make his way in the opposite direction from Mortwood, into the foothills of Castle Mount. It seemed a sensible enough option for a boy raised in the wilderness. Perhaps he would join the ranks of the great explorers of history. But it barely reached midmorning before Wally came to an imposing wall blocking his way.

It didn't appear to be an ordinary wall, at least not one made by men. It consisted of solid rock and reached higher than any wall he'd seen before. But it was too uniform and vertical to be natural. Running his hand over the coarse, pitted surface, Wally found it oddly warm for so early in the day. He backed up and studied the structure. It ran to his left and right as far as he could see. An urge to reach the other side overtook him. He'd never wanted anything as much as he wanted to get over that wall. He searched for a handhold and, finding a meager stub of rock, tried to grip it. No good.

Spotting a couple of cracks just wide enough to wedge his fingers, Wally pressed his soles against the wall at an angle and lifted his weight. Suddenly, his shoes gave way with a jolt, and his right knee crashed into the stone.

"Ow!" Wally cried as he crumpled to the ground. A flock of crows abandoned a nearby tree, cawing in protest. Angry at himself for making such a racket, he lay still for a time on the ground, holding his sore knee.

"You know, it's just an expression, right?" said a cheerful voice behind him.

Wally rolled around and looked up. A sturdy man smiled back. Dressed in a long, hooded robe cinched by a leather cord, he dangled a basket of dandelions and wild mushrooms from his right arm. At his left hung a long sword, its bejeweled hilt glinting in the sunshine.

"What is?" Wally asked feebly, as he folded up his pant leg to examine his swelling knee.

"No one really climbs Castle Wall," The man answered. "It's just a metaphor."

"Castle wall? There is a castle on the other side of the wall?" said Wally.

"You must have fallen harder than I thought. Are you okay, son?" said the man.

"I'm fine." Wally answered quietly.

"You're not from around here, are you, son?"

Wally froze, unsure whether to answer.

The man decided not to ask any more questions. "We call it Castle Wall. Some people consider it sacred. You may see people stand before it with their hands pressed against the granite, heads bowed. In Mortinburg, when one is said to have 'climbed Castle Wall' it means they have passed on."

"You mean . . ." Wally hesitated.

"They've died, yes."

Wally examined the wall again. "But . . . it's just a wall. All it would take is some rope or some structure—like a scaffold—to get over it. Certainly someone has tried," Wally said.

The man laughed kindly and shook his head. "Not who've lived to tell."

"There isn't a gate?" Wally asked, clearly amazed.

"There is only one way in." The man drew his index finger across his neck and made a pained expression. Then, smiling again he said, "Well, I have got to attend to my chores. But first, a breakfast of quail eggs and wild mushrooms. Hungry? I wouldn't mind the company."

"No. Thank you. I'm fine," Wally said, despite his rumbling stomach. He picked himself up, limping a little.

"Good luck with your adventure, son. But please, leave the wall. You are only going to hurt yourself." The man eyed Wally's battered knee. "More than you already have."

Wally watched the man wander out of sight, singing a pleasantly lilting tune as he went.

The bards are mute, the songs unsung
But you are not forgotten.
The waters hum, "Dear children, come,

The King waits in the mist!"
So, gather in, our joys begin
The King waits in the mist!

Wally faced the towering formation. Even more now, he wanted to see beyond it. He decided to follow the wall to the left in search of an opening. It was not an easy task. The ground some distance in front of the wall had been left wild and overgrown. Stumbling, Wally cursed the stones, big as bullfrogs, which seemed to hide spitefully under the shaggy grass. A spiderweb occasionally wrapped his face, snapping behind him as he ducked a bit too late. Prickly vines grabbed at the jacket Wally had stolen from the Mercantile. Luckily, the trousers he grabbed from the shelves fit him well, and his shoes were no longer covered in bacon grease.

Wally walked for longer than he expected. The sun reached its height and continued its western journey. Hours passed. Twisting and jarring, his ankles ached from the unevenness of the ground. His knee throbbed. More hours passed, and Wally began to lose enthusiasm for his adventure.

The daylight waned, and the cool air threatened to turn colder. Driven to find a break in the wall, he'd neglected to prepare for nightfall. A full day with little to eat had weakened him. What was he doing? He thought of home and the steady, predictable days in the Wood with Haden: early morning hunts; midday chores working hard side by side; warm venison and root stews in the evening followed by star gazing from the porch swing. Good memories. His face grew hot, and his throat cramped.

Just as he was thinking of quitting the wall, a low rushing sound caught his attention. As he continued, the sound grew into a roar.

A river! Of course! Wally thought. He could follow the river beyond the wall. Waljan's pace quickened. When he arrived at the waterway, his spirits fell.

A white, frothing mass of water tore through a large gap in Castle Wall. With frightening force, it tumbled and crashed against massive granite boulders. The breach in the wall seemed strangely intentional, its surface bending back and climbing with the waterline. And yet, the entire formation looked completely natural and wild.

Intensely curious, Wally craned his neck. But no matter how he tried, he could not actually see anything that lay beyond. He thought he might see better from a boulder in the center of the falls, but he couldn't find a way to get there. He stepped closer.

The spray of the falls blanketed Wally in mist. Shivering, he blew into his hands and tried to rub the chill from his stiff fingers. It helped a little. Ahead of him, the ground cut away sharply to a dangerous drop. Perhaps, he thought, there was a jutting root that would ease him down. Wally approached the edge of the falls only to be grabbed by the shoulder and abruptly spun around.

"Are you trying to murder yourself, Boy?" Haden asked, grasping both of Wally's shoulders in his thick, leathery hands. A look filled Haden's eyes that Wally had never seen before. It made Wally ashamed but sympathetic at the same time. Haden seemed to carry all the worry the world could know. Before Wally realized how much his own exhaustion, frustration, and love for Haden softened him, he fell into Haden's arms and started to cry.

"How did you find me?" Wally asked, sobbing.

"How can you ask me such a question? Aren't I the one who taught you to track?"

"Oh," Wally said with a snuffly chuckle. "Yeah."

"Don't you realize how worried I was about you? What are you doing out here?"

"I am sorry, Sir. I know I shouldn't have left."

"That river would swallow you up."

"I just wanted to get a closer look."

"Well that was too close. You must come back with me," Haden pleaded. "I've spoken to Mrs. Pruitt, and she is willing to forget the whole thing."

"Well, I'm not," Wally said, wiping the dirty wet streaks from his face. "It's easy to forget when you are the one causing trouble."

"What choice do you have? Where else can you go?" Haden reasoned.

"I want to see what's on the other side of Castle Wall," Wally answered.

Haden laughed through his own tears. "Oh, Wally, you are a piece of work." Then, he continued as if Wally hadn't even mentioned Castle Wall. "Look, Mrs. Pruitt may be as prickly as a cactus, but she fed you and let you sleep in a warm bed at night. It is more than I can do right now. But I have talked to Josiah Constance, and he thinks he can find you some work around the shop as long as you are not a bother. He will pay Mrs. Pruitt for your room at the house. You won't need to work for her anymore. And we can see each other every day."

"But what about the wall, Sir?" Wally asked.

Haden's brow fell and pinched right above his nose. "The wall? Oh! You're serious. Well, I'm sure we can find someone in Mortinburg who can tell you everything you want to know about Castle Wall . . . like that nice old lady that takes such an interest in you!" Haden chuckled as he shook his head.

"That's not funny, Sir!"

Haden assumed a graver expression. "No. It's not. You're right, Boy. Maybe I haven't wanted to admit to myself how difficult this move would be for you. Forgive me."

Wally sighed in resignation. "Only if you can forgive me for making it worse."

"Done. Now, help me get a fire going. Looks like we're camping out tonight."

10
Somewhere Else

SILENTLY and dutifully, Wally wiped down the empty shelves at the Mercantile. He stocked them with jars of vegetables, all lined up tidily with their labels facing straight out. Then, he swept the floor and refilled the grain bins. When his tasks were complete, Wally hunted down Mr. Constance.

"All done, Sir."

"Already? Well, good work, Waljan. Give me one second, and I will have something else for you to do. Mr. Constance reached in his pocket and pulled out a key ring attached to his belt by a chain. Charms, baubles, and glass beads overburdened the ring and swung restlessly, sending glints of yellow and red light around the room. Mr. Constance found the needed key and locked a little safe that sat under the counter. "I am going to lunch, and Haden should be back any minute from his. I need you to hold on to these keys until he returns. In the meantime, take this duster and shake it out thoroughly." Mr. Constance handed Wally the keys and the fluffy wool duster and pointed toward the front door.

An immediate sense of dread washed over Wally. He studied the open door and caught a slight glimpse of the hag around the corner. "Sir, I think it would be better to take it out back, where there aren't any customers coming and going."

"Good thinking. But keep an ear out."

This was the longest conversation Wally had managed at the Mercantile since starting there. The most he typically said was, "Yes, sir" or "Good morning, ma'am." Even with Haden, Wally was unusually quiet at work.

"I am worried about him," Haden had said to Mr. Constance recently.

"Wally is doing just fine," Mr. Constance replied. "He's a hard worker. Probably just focused. Still settling in."

"But something is not right, Josiah," Haden replied. "He's not usually this withdrawn."

But to Josiah, a quiet worker who got his work done well was a benefit to the store. He preferred things just as they were. As he headed out for his lunch break, Mrs. Pruitt entered with her sons. Haden came in from his lunch break right behind her.

"Mrs. Pruitt . . . hello, boys. What can I help you with?" Mr. Constance asked.

"Nothing, thank you, Josiah. I just thought Wally would like to have brought his lunch today. I took the time to prepare him a meal; you would think he'd remember to bring it with him."

"Well, Mrs. Pruitt," Haden offered, "you know there is a lot on his mind these days."

"True enough," she replied.

"He's out back, ma'am," said Mr. Constance. "You can take it right out to him."

Mrs. Pruitt directed her boys to take the sack she prepared out to Wally. They found him beating the duster against a storage barrel. With a sudden "Catch, Lodger!" Caddock tossed the sack at Wally, who flinched and flung the duster clear across the yard. The boys laughed. He glared at them.

"It's just lunch," Tyre said, finally in control of his giggles. Wally remained stony silent.

"Well, aren't you going to thank us?" Caddock added.

Wally opened the bag to find several clumps of grassy soil. Caddock broke out in raucous laughter as Wally tossed the bag aside.

"Cad! What did you do?" Tyre scolded, batting his brother in the stomach. "Wally, seriously, I thought it was in there. I saw Mom pack it." Tyre squirmed.

"Yeah. It was really delicious," added Caddock, sniggering.

"Caddock, knock it off!" Tyre tried to suppress his laughter, but failed.

Wally ignored them and retrieved the duster. But he seethed inside. With each petty prank Wally built up a quiet anger like a sleeping volcano.

"Aw, Tyre. The Shifty Lodger is pouting. You think we're due for another talking to from Mother?"

"Let's just go, Cad. He's not going to tell on us."

As the rogues took their leave, Wally retreated into his work. He tried to crowd thoughts of the twins out of his mind with daydreams about what adventure lay beyond Castle Wall. Haden had to say his name several times before Wally realized he was no longer alone.

"Where have you gone, Wally? It's like you're in another world."

"Oh, I am sorry, Sir."

"I wanted you to know that I am back from lunch, and I need the keys."

"Oh yeah . . .uh," Wally patted down his pockets and scanned the yard hastily. "There. Next to the door."

"What's wrong, Boy? Boys giving you trouble again?"

"No more than usual. It's nothing, Haden. It's just . . . I can't help it. I can't get that wall out of my mind."

"I see," said Haden and then handed Wally an apple. "Tyre Pruitt asked me to give this to you."

Wally didn't take it. "It's probably poisoned."

"No, he just bought it inside. I think it's a peace offering."

Wally thought a moment. He took the apple and took a bite.

"Come inside a moment," Haden suggested. "There is someone I think you should meet."

Wally followed Haden to the store's counter where a customer gathered a handful of candles and placed them gently in a basket. Wally immediately recognized the brown robe, bejeweled sword hilt, and warm expression.

"So, this is the Wally you've been telling me about," the man said.

Haden nodded and said, "Waljan Woodland, this is Sir Moriel of the Realm. He is a good friend of mine and would like to talk to you."

Wally said nothing but eyed the sparkling hilt of Moriel's magnificent sword.

"How about, 'Hello, nice to meet you, sir' as the first order of business, hmm?" Haden scolded.

"Oh, we've met, Haden," the man said. "By Castle Wall as a matter of fact."

"Oh?" said Haden in surprise.

Moriel continued, "It's called 'Paraclete,' Wally. Would you like to see it?"

"Huh? Well, yeah! Or no, sir, thank you. I'm working. Didn't you want to talk to me about something?"

Haden cut in, "I will cover you for a bit, Boy. Go take a break with Sir Moriel."

Moriel motioned for Wally to follow him out to the street.

Wally hesitated. "Must we talk there? There is someone out there, an old hag."

"Allie? Oh, she's harmless," Moriel assured him, and the two headed out onto the wooden walkway.

"Are you going to tell me to forget about the wall, sir?" Wally asked.

"It's not so easily done, is it?" Moriel replied.

"No, sir, it isn't."

"There is a reason for that, Wally," Moriel replied. "Most people don't sense what you sense. You've been called." Moriel looked around thoughtfully before continuing. "We are all children of the Realm, but many of us have forgotten our real home. And some of us just know—deep inside where nothing can twist the truth—that we belong somewhere else. Somewhere that isn't here."

"I don't understand, sir," Wally said.

"Haven't you heard any of the old Abidanian tales? Kings and knights and glorious deeds?"

"Well sure. Haden's told me lots of stories like that. But I don't see what that has to do with anything."

"Don't you?" Moriel probed.

"Of course he doesn't!" said a husky voice that emerged from around the corner. "He's too smart to fall for your fairy tales about magical lands behind Castle Wall."

A small gang of rough-looking men strutted past Moriel and encircled Wally. The leader and smallest of the pack spoke.

"There is nothing beyond Castle Wall but death. A black pit of endless emptiness."

Then a man the others called Coleman added, "If you did manage to scale the wall, which no one has, you would be sucked into that chasm, gone forever. But then again, it may be fun to watch him try, huh fellas?"

The motley gang laughed maliciously as Moriel forced his way through them to Wally's side.

"Okay, boys, you have had your fun. It's time to move on," Moriel said.

"No, we don't think so," said the leader. "You see, Asmodeus gave us orders to keep the folks in line around here, and we've gotten complaints about you."

"What complaints?" Moriel asked.

"Well, for one that you're recruiting young Mortinburgans, like this kid here, to some kind of secret army. You know, corrupting the minds of the young."

"Telling curious minds about the traditions and histories of Mortania is hardly a crime, my friends," Moriel replied with an easy charm.

"Just know that we are watching you. And we are not your friends," the man warned.

"Gentlemen!" A pleading interruption came from the other side of the street. Judge Asmodeus crossed over and joined the gang. Wally recognized him as the owner of the ruby pendant. "Officer Malvo, now what is this about? Is there some trouble?"

"Nah, boss, just keeping the peace like you asked."

"Very well then, on your way. I would like to speak with Sir

Moriel of the Realm privately. But meet me back in the office when you have finished your rounds," said Asmodeus.

Wally realized he'd hardly been breathing and let out a relieved sigh as the gang reluctantly moved on.

Asmodeus watched them go and then turned to Moriel. "That is what they call you, am I right? Sir Moriel of the Realm? A curious title."

"To those who are unfamiliar with it, certainly, Your Honor."

The judge faced Wally. "And this is young . . . Waljan, correct?"

"Forgive me, Judge," Moriel said in tightly controlled words, "but this is not a good time for us to visit."

"But Sir Moriel, isn't that exactly what you and the boy are doing? Visiting? And in a public space, no less. I would think that if you intended on privacy you would have met elsewhere."

"Your Honor, we do have a legal right to chat on the walkway, am I correct?" asked Moriel.

"Well, that does depend on what you are chatting about, doesn't it?" Asmodeus dropped his gentlemanly pretense. "That wall is dangerous. You wouldn't want Wally to vanish behind it." Asmodeus studied Moriel's undaunted expression, and backed off. "But, I suppose . . ."

"YOU!" The guttural, raspy exclamation erupted from a ragged lump below the walk. Wally's tormentor leapt up and galloped toward the three. Before Wally knew what was happening, Moriel instinctively pulled Wally out of the way. The hag threw herself against Asmodeus, fists flying wildly.

"You crazy shrew!" Asmodeus exclaimed as he grappled with her flailing arms and finally thrust her hard to the ground. He took a step toward her, but Moriel gently took hold of his arm.

"This overreaction doesn't suit a man of your rank, Your Honor," Moriel rebuked.

"Overreaction? Sir, I have been assaulted!" Asmodeus ripped his arm from Moriel's grasp. "I am not done with you, dog!" he hissed at the crouching woman. The judge straightened his coat with a jerk and dusted the silk topper that had fallen to the ground. Turning to Moriel he added, "I decide what is becoming a man of my rank. You should thank me for protecting your young friend from this woman."

"I doubt we had much to fear from Allie, Your Honor," Moriel replied.

"Well, you may have something to fear from me, sir. I expect to see you in my office tomorrow to answer for several complaints that have been made about you. Good day." Asmodeus tramped off, adding over his shoulder, "And since you are taking responsibility for her, get that crazy shrew off the street!"

Moriel eased the old woman up from her cowering huddle. "Are you all right? Now what was that about? Come, sit down."

But the woman avoided his gestures and kept her head down. She broke away from his gentle hands and scooted quickly down the walkway. As she turned the corner, Haden appeared in the doorway.

"Is everything okay?" he asked.

"With us, it is. I'm not so sure it is with that one," Moriel replied facing the direction Allie had retreated. "I wish someone could help her."

"She's a frightful witch," Wally said under his breath.

"She's a human being, Wally," Moriel scolded sharply.

"Forgive me, sir, but she just attacked us for no reason!" Wally's frightened eyes fixed on Moriel.

"No, son. I don't think her anger was directed at us." Moriel thought a moment. "We should continue our discussion another day. Think about what I said."

11
Hooligans

ASMODEUS slammed his hands on his oversized cherry wood desk. "I did not tell you to make a nuisance of yourselves, harassing the townspeople and implicating me in your stupidity!"

"But, boss . . ." Malvo protested. Bruce Malvo was head of Asmodeus's private security force. Small and lean, but mean like a terrier, his silky black curls framed a rectangular face that would be handsome if not for its weathered, bubbly complexion.

Asmodeus interrupted with a hiss, "It is not your place to question my orders, but to carry them out!"

"Yes, sir," Malvo replied, his tone dripping with resentment. He and his accomplices exchanged exasperated glances.

Asmodeus sighed. "To you, these are harmless people. Weak. Mild. They are store clerks. Washerwomen. Ranchers. Ordinary folk. But these people are more powerful than even they realize. They serve an enemy you do not know nor understand, and I will not let him win." The judge calmed himself, tugging on the tails of his silk vest and straightening his bow tie.

Asmodeus elegantly raised his gloved index finger in emphasis, adding, "We need finesse, not force. Waljan is just an awkward, struggling little orphan. But I have seen into that boy's heart.

There is a frightening strength there. Little problems become big problems if you let them. Now, I want to know what Moriel is up to at all times, and from now on, in secret. Do you understand?" The men nodded. "Good. I will take care of Waljan Woodland. He is mine already. I have a special gift prepared just for him."

"So . . ." Krass, an overlarge, droopy-eyed hooligan, interjected. "I don't get it. You're gonna get rid of the kid by giving him a gift? Gonna 'kill 'em with kindness' as they say?" He grunted out a heavy chuckle.

"No, you ape. I am not going to get rid of him at all. Does that thing that sits between your shoulders serve a purpose, or is it just for decoration?"

"What thing, boss?" Krass asked.

"Never mind," Asmodeus said. "The best way to make a problem go away is to solve it."

Krass puzzled over Asmodeus's words. "Why don't you give us gifts, boss?"

"Open your shirt, Krass," Asmodeus commanded.

"Huh?" Krass replied.

Asmodeus marched over to the muscle-bound man and ripped his shirt open, sending buttons ricocheting around the room. An ugly, gray goat skull tattoo adorned the left side of the man's bulky chest. "What do you think THAT is?"

"A tattoo?" Krass asked, unsure of the judge's point.

Asmodeus donned a smile of bemused disbelief. "A gift, you oaf."

"Oh. I was kind of hoping for a—"

Before Krass could say another word, Malvo kicked him hard in the side of his shin.

"Leave. You all have work to do," Asmodeus said with bored

disdain. After they left the room, the judge retrieved his signature mahogany gift box from the bottom drawer of his desk. The goat skull seal emblazoned on the box lid flashed in the light as he raised it, revealing a gold compass. He lifted the compass and gently placed it upside down on the desk.

From a little leather pouch, Asmodeus grabbed a pair of tweezers and a flat piece of metal he used to pry open the back of the compass. He then opened a handkerchief that he kept in his coat pocket. Nestled in its folds were a number of heart-shaped gems of various sizes. With the tweezers, the judge lifted a particularly small heart from the cache and placed it gingerly into the back of the compass. Then he snapped the casing back together and flipped it over. Where the N would typically reside, the ruby peeked through a heart-shaped cutout. Like a proud artist putting the last touches on a masterpiece, Asmodeus tucked the compass firmly into the gift box's cushioned interior.

* * * * *

All week, Wally dwelt on Moriel's strange words. While he stocked the pickle shelves, the questions rattled around in his head. *We are children of the Realm?* Loading customers' carts he puzzled over the words. *We belong somewhere else?* Sweeping the floors at the end of the day, he pondered. *What did he mean?* He asked Haden, but that didn't help much.

"Wally, I can teach you the proper way to hook up a carriage. I can show you the difference between the tracks made by a lame animal versus a healthy one. I can teach you just about any knot known to man. But there is a reason I asked Moriel to visit you. I am just no good at these big questions of life. I am a practical man. A doer. Not a thinker. Have patience. I know Moriel will answer your questions next time he is in town."

As he walked home one evening, Wally came across Asmodeus out on a park bench watching the stars. The judge seemed out of place. Wally approached, avoiding eye contact.

"So, young troublemaker, what mischief do you have planned for tonight?" Asmodeus asked.

"Mischief, Your Honor? I am just walking home. I don't want any trouble," Wally said as he continued walking.

Asmodeus leapt to his feet and caught up to the boy. "You are entirely too sensitive, Waljan. You act as if I am insulting you."

"I don't understand," Wally protested. "I'm sorry, but I need to get home."

"Why do you think being a troublemaker is such a bad thing? No one is perfect. In fact, my job would be downright boring if we were."

"So, you think I should cause trouble so that your job will be more fun?" Wally said, perplexed. He began to walk faster.

Asmodeus let out a loud guffaw. "Oh, Waljan, I like you."

Wally stopped and turned to face the judge. "You do?"

"Why, certainly! You're funny. Full of grit and acid. It's lovely."

Wally felt unexpectedly pleased at this. And it bothered him. Asmodeus was the most respected man in the city, polished and handsome. But there was something about him that made Wally's palms sweat and his back squirm. The judge embodied contradiction. He was both intriguing and repulsive, charming but alarming. And the current conversation did not seem that of a lawman.

Asmodeus stared intently at Waljan. "I have something for you. Think of it as a thank-you for returning my pendant. That was a priceless trinket I thought I'd lost forever." Asmodeus handed Wally the mahogany box.

Wally opened it and peered in. "What is it?"

"Wha . . ." Asmodeus sputtered. "What is it? Why, it's a compass, Wally. As a woodland boy surely you've used a compass before!"

"No. What does it do?"

Asmodeus laughed at the boy's simplicity. "It tells you what direction you're going, north, south, east, west . . . so you don't get lost in the wilderness." Asmodeus laid heavy emphasis on his next comment, which struck Wally as oddly unnecessary. "It is important to know the right way to go, Waljan."

"I always know which way to go, Your Honor. The forest tells me. And when I'm not in the forest, the sun does. I never get lost." Wally handed the box back to Asmodeus, but the judge wouldn't take it.

"At least take it out of the box and look at it," Asmodeus suggested.

Reluctantly, Wally popped the compass out of its box and held it in the palm of his hand. The ruby at "north" gleamed blood red. Suddenly, a deep longing for home inundated him, and his eyes pooled. With alarm, he recalled feeling this before, the day he delivered the ruby pendant. Embarrassed by his uncontrollable emotion, Wally abruptly thrust the compass in the judge's direction. "Here, please take it."

"You don't understand, Wally. It's yours. It's a gift."

"That is very kind of you, but I can't accept such a gift," Wally said, his voice cracking.

"But why not? It is just a token of appreciation. You deserve it." Asmodeus held his serene gaze momentarily. A leering expression replaced it. "Oh . . . You don't trust me. I understand. I am supposed to be all about the law—rules and order and maintaining the peace. I listen to people's complaints and serve out punishments for bad behavior. Yes, I do. And I know more than anyone that it is natural for people to cause trouble. If it weren't, my services as judge would not be necessary. But you think all that doesn't apply to you. Tell me, Waljan, why do you think yourself so much better than anyone else?"

"What? I don't!" Wally argued. Still holding the compass awkwardly, his extended hand shook and his face grew hot.

"Of course you do. If you're too high and mighty to accept a gift of appreciation from one of the most important men in town, I need no other proof. But I'll give you another example anyway. You let those Pruitt boys walk all over you. They know that you would forgive all and become friends if only they would let you. But they don't. Their snide comments, their nasty pranks—snakes in your bed, salt in your water jug—they do these things just to see you annoyed, shamed, hurt."

"How do you know abou—" Wally interjected, but Asmodeus barreled on.

"And what do you do? Nothing. Because you are too good to respond. They deserve a response. But you hold back because good boys don't seek revenge."

Wally did not know how to reply even if he could through his sobs. He decided not to try. Instead, he dropped the compass at Asmodeus's feet and ran as fast as he could toward home. Asmodeus watched him go, thinking aloud, "It's either corruption or destruction, my dear Waljan. The choice is yours."

12
Troubleshooting

GEEZ slammed his palm on the bar counter and pointed his knobbly, quivering finger a few inches from Bruce Malvo's nose. "The likes of you are not going to harass my customers, do you understand, Malvo?"

Wally looked on, concerned that the old man's impressive courage would not end well. He and Moriel had come in for lunch. Wally asked Moriel to answer some of the questions that lingered from their last conversation, and Moriel suggested stopping by Geezer's Geyser.

Geez continued, "Now you get your filthy, no-good gangsters out of my restaurant."

Moriel quietly sent Waljan out on an errand, worried about the rising tension. Then, he responded to the fuming Geez with silky calm, "Gerald. Relax. This isn't your fight."

"Isn't it? With all due respect, Sir Moriel, this isn't about you. I know you can handle yourself against these delinquents. But what about the others? I've been lying low, trying to avoid these guys. Cowering over here behind the counter thinking that if I stayed out of their way they would leave me alone. I've never wanted any trouble. But now they're in here coming after my customers. Last week it was a young couple having lunch with their children. They were somehow 'disturbing the peace' because the baby was a little hungry and fussing about it. Yesterday it was an old woman, in 'possession of controlled material.' Her crime was reading Mortanian history while sipping her afternoon tea."

"And today, it might be you, old man," Malvo announced through gritted teeth. "Interfering with an officer of the law. We are going to take Moriel in for questioning, and there is nothing you can do about it."

"You're no officer of the law, and I can still throw a punch, little punk," Geez derided the thug. "And I can suffer a few broken bones to give you a piece of my mind."

Moriel intervened. "Whoa, hold on, Geez. I have no problem going with the gentlemen. Let's just save your energy for something more important, okay? Please, just take care of the customers and don't worry. I got this."

"Now wait just a minute, Moriel," said Malvo as his companions Krass, Bader, and Coleman moved slowly behind the bar counter and toward the old proprietor. "I am taking you both in. But not before I teach this mouthy codger a lesson."

The men grabbed Geez, who immediately started to throw punches and insults left and right. Though the insults hit their mark, Geez's fists met nothing but air as the men dragged him out of the restaurant and threw him into the street. They surrounded him like a pack of hyenas.

On his way back from the herbalist's shop, Wally nearly walked into the middle of the conflict. The men didn't notice him. They were too busy toying with poor Geez and laughing. Geez scrambled to retrieve the opalescent rock that had rolled out of his pocket when he hit the ground. The men let him nearly reach it before kicking it away again. Wide-eyed, Wally dropped the package that Moriel had sent him for but really didn't need. The lemon mint cough lozenges exploded from the bag and bounced around in the dirt.

"What are you doing?" Waljan screamed, "Leave him alone!" Wally tried to run to Geez's side, but Krass grabbed him by the arm and nearly lifted Wally off the ground.

"That's enough!" came Moriel's booming command. He strode into the middle of the gang, freed Wally from Krass's grip, and then put his arm around Geez Guest. "I want all of you to clear out of here. I am taking Geez back into the restaurant. Come on, Wally."

With a resounding crack Moriel lurched back in pain. Malvo stood with a black leather whip in his hands. "By whose authority do you tell me what to do?"

Moriel straightened up. "Wally. Don't be afraid. Calmly walk Mr. Guest back into the restaurant." When Wally had cleared the circle of thugs and escorted Geez safely inside, Moriel drew his sword, Paraclete, and pointed it directly toward Bruce Malvo. "Leave now by the authority of the King of Abidan."

"Really?" Malvo laughed. "Are you kidding me? Is this why you dress up in a blanket and carry a sword? What a loony!"

The goons joined in with snickers and jabs. After bowing deeply and reverently in jest, Malvo cracked his whip high in the air, saying, "Well, Sir Moriel, I am going to enjoy snapping you back to reality." He circled the whip around and sent the leather braid flying toward Moriel's head.

Wally exited the restaurant just in time to witness Moriel pivot gracefully with both hands on his hilt and come up from under the striking whip, slicing the end off and sending the tip spinning away. The end that Malvo still controlled fell limply to the ground. Reflexively, Moriel stomped hard, trapping it. Wally wanted to yell, "Bravo!" but thought better of it. Malvo clutched the whip handle, frozen at what he'd just seen. The laughing and jesting stopped in an instant. It reminded Wally of the frogs at the polliwog pond in Mortwood, and he chuckled to himself.

Moriel sheathed Paraclete and raised his hands in the air. "Now," he said, "I am ready to go meet with the judge. You may escort me as gentlemen. Not as henchmen. Asmodeus doesn't need to know about any of this. But you are going to leave Gerald Guest and the good citizens of this town alone. Is that clear?"

The four hooligans nodded silently and as casually as they could, now knowing the real threat that Moriel presented.

"Wally!" Moriel called. "See yourself back to the Pruitt's. I will meet you there when I am through."

All the way home, Wally replayed Moriel's heroics and the cruelty of Asmodeus's men. He wondered what drove them to target people like Gerald Guest. Humble people. Good people. Then he recalled the stone. Geez tried to recover his dropped stone as if it were more precious than his own life. Wally had to know why.

Retrieving the sap-covered stone from his desk drawer, Wally hustled downstairs in search of Mrs. Pruitt. She was in the parlor, sewing the last delicate rosebud into a tablecloth with silky fuchsia thread.

"There," she said, satisfied. "What do you think, Waljan?" She spread the tablecloth out over the sofa and admired it proudly.

"It's very nice, ma'am," Wally said politely.

"Thank you. Now, did you need something, dear?"

"Yes, ma'am. I hope you don't mind, but I found something upstairs in my room, and I was hoping you could tell me what it is." Wally held out his open hand to reveal the stone. He had managed to clean off the sap, leaving the surface beautifully radiant. It nearly glowed.

"Where did you find that?" Mrs. Pruitt gasped. She looked at it first with longing, reaching out with a trembling hand. Then with sudden loathing, she smacked the stone out of Wally's hand and across the room. "That is a very dangerous object, Waljan. You stay away from anyone who has one, uses one, talks about one. Do you hear me?"

Wally was stunned. "Uh . . . yes, ma'am. But . . . what is it?"

A knock at the door interrupted them. From the other side Moriel shouted, "Mrs. Pruitt, is everything all right in there?"

Josephine Pruitt strutted over to the door and threw it open. "No. It is not, sir!" She pointed in the corner of the room where the stone had fallen. Tears now filled her eyes. "Please take care of that," she pleaded and ran up the stairs.

Filled with compassion, Moriel approached the stone. Wally felt like he was in a strange dream. Nothing seemed to make any sense.

"Come back to me!"

"What did you say, Moriel?" Wally asked, the hair on his arms bristling.

Moriel glanced over to Wally. "I said nothing, Wally. What did you hear?"

"Uh . . . nothing I guess . . . I . . . must have heard someone outside." Wally nodded as if reassuring himself.

Picking up the stone reverently, Moriel pulled a soft cloth

from a pouch that hung at his waist. He wrapped the stone up tenderly and tucked it away. Sighing deeply, he crossed his arms and leaned back against the wall as if drained of energy.

"I'm sorry," Wally said. "I don't know what is happening here. I just wanted to know what that was."

"Oh, Wally, please," Moriel said. "There is no way you could have anticipated any of that. This is not your fault. It's a story that I can't get into now, and certainly not here." He pushed himself away from the wall and walked over to Wally. "We have other things to talk about." Moriel patted Wally on the shoulder.

"What you did for Mr. Guest was . . . it was incredible, sir," Wally said with awe in his eyes.

"No, Waljan. What you did for Mr. Guest was incredible. I have a sword. Training. Years of battles, conflicts, victories under my belt. You came to Mr. Guest's aid with nothing but the desire to help a vulnerable old man in need. Yours was the greater act of courage."

Wally beamed. "Thank you, sir."

"Now, why don't you spend some of that courage on preparing a nice, soothing cup of soup for Mrs. Pruitt. I think she could use something warm and comforting about now."

"I'll try, sir, but it will take an act of courage for her to eat it," Wally replied and headed toward the kitchen.

13
Home

"SIT down, Waljan!" Haden snipped. "One good jolt will knock you clean off the rig."

The wagon tripped and stumbled over the rocky path that the Longbows called "Wit's End Road." They couldn't have picked a more pleasant morning for a visit in the Wood. The sun rose into a cloudless sky that morning, but the cool autumn breeze kept the temperatures mild.

"But I can just about see their place, Haden!" Wally said, brimming with joy and anticipation. A protective bark echoed from up the hill, warning the visitors that they'd been discovered. "I'll save you the worry and just jump off here," Wally added, leaping from the cart and darting up the road as quickly as the loose stones would allow.

A blur of golden fur, flapping ears, and galloping paws shot toward Wally like a rocket, barking and whimpering the whole way.

"Bo Dog! Buddy! It's me!" Wally crouched down and opened his arms to catch the animal that hurdled headlong into them. Bo knocked Wally clean off his feet and covered his face with warm, smelly kisses. He tap-danced and scooted and waggled with more energy than a fish out of water. Wally giggled like a boy half his age.

"You're huge, Bo! What has Peep been feeding you?" The dog howled an answer that Wally could not translate, and then scurried off toward the house. He stopped short, turned, and barked back to Wally as if they were late for a royal ceremony. Wally followed, beaming with a smile he couldn't remove if he tried. By the time he and Bo reached the house, Haden had already passed them and was drawing in Maggie's reins beside the porch. Haden jumped down and tied the reins to a post.

"He missed you," Haden said warmly while he scratched Bo behind the ears.

"Yeah," Wally replied.

The front door swung open, and Cullie came out to welcome his guests. Penelope pushed around him, sprinting, and sprang off the porch, clearing all five steps. "Wally!" she squealed, startling poor Haden. Her feet barely hit the ground before she grabbed Wally's hands and pulled him toward the forest. "Come on, come on! I have to show you something!" As they ran off she grabbed a bulging sack tied to a long stick and flung it over her shoulder. In an instant they were gone through a wall of branches that lazily sprang back into place behind them.

"Wow!" Haden exclaimed.

Cullie smiled back at him, serenely, with one hand resting in his pocket and the other wrapped around a steaming mug of coffee. Cullie always took things in stride. He was a rock against which the storm waves of Penelope's life crashed. He had always been mature for his age. And when his parents died, he assumed the mantle of father, mother, protector, and confidante as naturally as if he had trained for the role.

"There is fresh coffee in the house, and some kind of cake," Cullie offered. "At least I think it's cake. Penelope made it. It's probably edible."

"Well, coffee sounds wonderful!" Haden replied.

While the men caught up, Wally, Penelope, and Bo sprawled out over the heated surface of Promise Rock, swapping news of their own.

"Look, Wally! Look what I found!" Penelope said. She was a tightly wound spring ready to burst with excitement. Penelope unwrapped her pack and withdrew a little painting on pine board. She handed it to Wally. A beautiful woman with large chestnut eyes, a soothing smile, and red curly locks tied up under a bonnet looked past him from the painting.

"That's your mom, Peep! See? She looks just like you. Now you will never forget her. Where did you get this?"

"Cullie found it under a floorboard in the house with a bunch of drawings and pencils and some old letters to Ma. Apparently, Dad was an artist! I had never known that."

"Wow. That is really great, Peep. I'm glad you found that. What else did you bring in that pack?" Wally asked, curiously. He hadn't eaten since early that morning, and his stomach felt like it was imploding.

"A picnic!" Peep flipped open a folded blanket to spread over the rock's surface. On it she laid two wooden mugs, a canteen of water, and a pair of napkins. Then, she set out a feast of apples, boiled eggs, hard cheese, jerky, and something that resembled cake. Triumphantly Penelope announced, "There! I made it all myself. Try the cake, Wally!"

Starving, Wally bit into the pastry. His teeth sank in and then slogged through as if slicing half-dried clay. Wally's taste buds revolted and the inner lining of his mouth shriveled. "Iss weayie gud . . ." he said, trying to resist gagging. Penelope beamed.

Wally forced the lump of cake down with half a canteen of water. "I better save that for after lunch. I don't want to ruin my appetite!" he said.

When the friends finished their meal, they packed up their picnic and stretched out on the stone. The river slipped by lazily many feet below them. Wally thought to himself that it was a shame he didn't bring his fishing pole along. The cake that he was simply too full to finish would have made excellent bait. Not only would it have held together well in the water, but he wouldn't have needed a sinker. But there was enough to talk about that he really didn't need any other diversion.

"A hag! That is awesome!" The thought captivated Penelope's imagination.

"You have a weird sense of awesome, Peep." Wally replied.

"But having someone around to perform magic spells could be very convenient, Wally," Penelope advised. "Why haven't you ever told me about her before?"

"She's not a pet, Peep. She's not even a friend. She's scary, ugly, unpredictable, and smells like a bog. Why would I tell you about her?"

"But she's mysterious, Wally. I bet she has an interesting story!" Penelope argued.

"I doubt it. I am more interested in knowing what's behind Castle Wall," Wally confessed. He leapt off Promise Rock to a smaller boulder and then to the pebble-covered banks of Meander Creek. Sifting through the water-worn granite and basalt stones, Wally discovered the perfect one for skipping and bounced it off the top of the water with a flick of his elbow. Bo heard the rock slap across the water's surface and plop down to the river bed. He snapped his head toward the sound, and, catching sight of the ripples, bounded into the water in pursuit.

"Silly dog," Wally quipped.

Penelope grabbed her sack and followed Wally down to the bank. "What do you think is behind the wall?"

"Well, Castle Mount, for one thing. Everyone can see that. And where there is a mountain there is land and animals and people, right?" Wally took off his shoes and socks and waded to a tree that had fallen over the stream. Goose bumps shot up his legs, across his back, and over his shoulders. He straddled the log and let his feet dangle, submerged in the cold water. Then he continued. "Some say a kingdom lies on the peaks of Castle Mount, but no one has ever been there to prove it, nor has anyone from there come here."

"Fairy tales," Penelope interjected.

"Maybe. Others in town say that between the wall and the mountain there is a black pit that sucks you into an eternity of nothing."

"Maybe you should forget about the wall, Wally. I mean, if we were meant to know what is on the other side, wouldn't we already? Wouldn't somebody know? Sometimes curiosity is dangerous."

"Haden and his friend Sir Moriel seem to think it's dangerous. But when I was there, I didn't feel afraid. I felt like I belonged on the other side."

"Yeah. I think that's what scares me about it the most. Maybe your hag put a spell on it!"

Wally rolled his eyes and kicked a wave of water toward Penelope. She sprang away, giggling.

"Ha!" Peep hopped the stones that formed a natural bridge across the stream. "Last one back to the cabin sucks fish heads!"

"Wait!" Wally called to her. "I don't even have my shoes on yet!"

"Well, I guess you're going to lose, then!" Penelope shouted from behind the reeds that lined the opposite bank.

When Wally finally caught up to Penelope, she was already sitting on her porch sipping lemonade. By her breathlessness, he wasn't fooled into thinking she beat him by much. Haden and Cullie sat with her, amused by the friends' never-waning competitiveness. Wally joined the party, gulping down the lemonade that had been set out for him.

"We've come to a decision, Wally," Haden said. "Cullie has agreed to take you in."

"With the understanding, of course," added Cullie, "that you will contribute to the household. But I doubt that will be a problem for you."

"Really!" Wally exclaimed. Then, a rush of competing "ifs" and "thens" and "what-abouts" crowded his brain, battling for attention. His mouth could only manage a stutter.

Penelope giggled.

Wally forced it out. "I am really . . . are you sure, Cullie?"

"Of course I am, Wally," Culbert insisted. "We're already like family. It'll be a natural fit."

"It's settled then," Haden concluded.

The next day, Haden and Wally swung by their old cabin to pick up some things that had been left behind when they moved to town. As they drove up, the soothing comfort of familiarity overwhelmed Wally. *If only it could be as it was, just Haden and me,* he thought.

"We may have some critters to contend with," Haden warned. "They tend to move in when a place is left long enough."

Pensively, the two passed to the front door. Everything was frozen in time. Not a thing had been disturbed in all the months they'd been away. Remembering that he had some canned goods in the pantry, Haden grabbed a wooden crate from the porch and started loading it.

"Josephine could use these peaches, I expect. I hope they're still good. Oh! And those beans. Those were delicious, weren't they, Wally? You think she'd like those?"

Wally was only half listening. "Yeah, sure." He wandered from room to room. A cedar hobbyhorse with a mane and tail of unraveled hemp rope collected dust in the center of one room. Haden had carved it for Wally years ago. Fishing flies the two had tied together sat in a clay bowl that Wally made. Haden had taught him how to find the right grade of clay, and how to stack bricks to make a kiln hot enough to fire pottery. A quill full of arrows, prepped for a hunt that never came, waited by the back door.

Waljan called over to Haden, "Do you think we could take our bows target shooting one last time?"

Haden appeared from around the corner. "Of course, Boy."

14
Choices

THUNK! Haden's arrow hit the target just three inches from the center. "It's been too long since we've arched a bow, Wally. I'm losing my accuracy."

Thunk! Wally hit dead on. "Funny enough, I think I've gotten better!"

"Well, let's see you do that a few more times before you make that claim," Haden suggested.

Thunk! Another arrow ripped into the center of the target.

"How's that, Haden?" Wally laughed.

"Good work, Waljan. I think I'm done." Haden collected his arrows and sat down on a log, leaning his hands on his knees and breathing deeply.

"You all right?" Wally asked.

"Yeah. Just winded," Haden replied.

Wally sat down and waited silently for Haden to recover. He breathed in the forest. If only he could hold it in and keep it with him always—the deep love of the place, the memories, the calm—he would.

Overhead, a gang of crows screamed alarm. Haden looked up and huffed. "They never give up, those dumb birds."

Wally tracked the birds in their fruitless attempt at intimidation. A large hawk circled, soaring ever higher, undisturbed by the cawing and swooping that surrounded it. The bird of prey dodged and twisted with little effort. He remained forever at ease. Wally smiled at the thought of Moriel facing off against Asmodeus's men.

Almost without thinking, Wally slipped an arrow out of his quill and nocked his bow. The point of his arrow followed the lead crow, and then plunk! He let his arrow fly. In an eruption of feathers, the crow flipped and then spiraled down to the ground. The rest of the crows flew off in all directions, allowing the hawk to circle in peace.

"Are you planning on eating that, Wally?" Haden asked.

"No, Sir," Wally confessed. "I don't know why I did that."

"I heard about what happened with Mr. Guest and some of the judge's hired men. I also heard that you tried to help."

Wally remained silent, watching the hawk vanish into the blue.

"You don't have to worry about that anymore. You have your peaceful woodland life back."

"Yeah," Wally said. "But, it wasn't all bad. I mean, you were right. We don't have to see everything from underneath. I learned to read a little. I can write my name. Not that I will need that in the Wood, but still. Maybe I can teach Peep. I've met some good people. Been on some adventures."

"Oh, that you have!" Haden said, laughing. "Well, Boy. You can visit. Anytime. When I have saved enough money, I can send a horse. How's that?"

"No, Haden. That's your money."

"And what is an old codger like me gonna do with it, huh?

You got yourself a horse. Just gotta be patient. Okay?"

"Thank you, Sir," Wally replied.

Haden squeezed Wally's shoulder, looking away into the distance. "I am going to miss you more than you could know, Boy."

Wally nodded.

"Now, before I change my mind, let's get back to Cullie and Peep. We need time to unpack the rig before nightfall. I'm on my way back to town tomorrow."

Haden, Wally, Cullie, and Peep spent their last night together quietly and retired early. Haden and Wally settled down by the fireplace with Bo Dog nestled between them, and within minutes Haden was softly snoring and puffing. Wally couldn't sleep. He tossed. He beat his pillow and flipped it over. He watched the fire dance. Clear strands of heat gently slid off the tips of each flame and wriggled away.

Bo growled and lifted his head.

"What is it, boy?" Wally asked.

The dog ran to the door, whining and pawing.

"I've already let you out once, Bo. Are you going to do this all night?" But Wally relented and opened the door. The house vanished like clouds on a summer morning. Before Wally a giant rock face appeared, just like the wall that encircled Castle Mount, but not quite as high. Wally could see the top clearly and was certain that if he could reach it, he would be able to cross over to the other side easily.

"Come back to me!" a voice cried.

"Who are you?" Wally shouted.

A rope fell from the top of the wall, beckoning him. Wally began to climb. But the more he climbed, the higher the wall became. He climbed faster, trying to overcome the wall's growth. Before long he had cleared the treetops, the mountain peaks, and the cloud layer. Then, he moved into the dark of space. His hands cramped and burned against the rough fibers of the rope, and he grew increasingly tired. I just want to sleep. Let me sleep! he thought.

Suddenly, a murder of crows descended on Wally. They pecked at his face and hands and grabbed at him with their leathery feet. Wally couldn't hang on any longer. He dropped the rope and plummeted through the air, floating at first and then picking up speed. Faster and faster he fell until, shouting something incoherent, Wally threw off the covers and sat up with a start.

"You all right there, Wally?" Haden asked, sitting at the breakfast table. Cullie stood at the stove with a spatula in hand, staring at Wally, eyebrows raised. The rich, sweet smell of freshly brewed coffee mingled with the scent of fried quail eggs and sausage. "Breakfast is nearly ready."

Wally rubbed his face and sat a moment, hugging his knees. Then he rose to roll up the sleeping mat in his blankets. On his way to wash up he grunted, "Yeah . . . okay."

Breakfast was uncomfortably quiet. Difficult good-byes often are. Peep, usually the firecracker among them, was more like an ember. She had to suppress her enthusiasm for having Wally back, knowing how sad he and Haden were at their parting.

"It looks like you're going to have clear weather going back," Cullie said to Haden.

"Looks like," Haden agreed.

Wally poked at the wiggly yolk of his egg with his fork.

"You all loaded up?" Cullie asked.

"Think so," answered Haden.

Peep tossed bits of sausage over to Bo, who snapped them out of the air and right down his throat.

Finally, Wally tossed his fork on the table. "I can't stay here," he admitted.

Haden's mouth fell open. Cullie glanced from Wally to Haden and back again. Penelope's expression fell like a deflated balloon.

"What are you talking about?" Haden barked. Bo slinked under the table, tail lowered. "You know I would take you back with me in a heartbeat, Wally. But you have been badgering me about coming home for months. You begged me to stay here in the first place. You run from the Pruitt's home, hide from old Allie, fume over Caddock and Tyre, and now you want to go back after I finally agree to let you stay! What do you want from us, Wally? Please tell us because I can't figure you out anymore!" Haden glared at Wally, arms crossed, puffing from exasperation.

"I'm sorry. I know, and you're right," Wally said in the calmest, most reasonable tones he could manage. "You may never understand because I don't even understand. You three are the only family I have known. But Moriel said something to me that I can't shake. He said we belong somewhere else, that we have another home. And I realized that I have never really had a home in the first place. Not that you haven't been like a father, Haden, and you, Cullie and Peep, have been the best sister and brother anyone could ask for. But I really don't belong to any of you. I thought coming back to the Wood was coming home." Wally sighed and shook his head. "But I know now that home is somewhere else, and I have to find it. I want to go home."

Silence fell so thickly over the four that they could hear Bo's deep, sleepy breath from under the table. Tears soaked Penelope's face.

Cullie gently leaned forward and asked, "But if the Wood isn't home, Wally, and Mortinburg isn't home, what is?"

"I don't know. But the answer lies in Mortinburg. Not here."

"Okay, Wally," Haden finally said with a heaviness that Wally felt in the pit of his stomach, and didn't understand. "Let's load up and go."

As Maggie jerked the rig into action, carrying Haden and Wally down the hill and away from the Longbow's property, Cullie, Peep, and Bo watched them go. Cullie waved one last time, but Peep just stood with her arms crossed. Bo whimpered and howled. Finally, he broke away from the others and bolted down the hill barking woefully after the rig. But Maggie at a steady canter was too fast for him and, eventually Wally lost sight of the dog.

Part II

MERCY CALLS

15
Sanctuary

CHERRY blossoms flitted sleepily past the window pane like snow, carrying Wally's mind away with them. Winter had slogged by, wet and bracing, and finally loosed its grip.

"Waljan! Pay attention!" Mrs. Pruitt demanded.

Her student's eyes snapped back to the book that lay before them. "I'm sorry, Mrs. Pruitt. It's just such a beautiful day."

"The days are getting longer and warmer. Surely you have time to enjoy them without disrupting your lessons."

A sharp rapping echoed down the hall.

"Oh my, the time has slipped away from me! That must be Justice Asmodeus here for our appointment. Waljan, do you mind completing this lesson tomorrow?"

"Oh, not at all, ma'am," Wally said hastily, flipping his book closed and popping out of his chair.

"Oh, thank you, dear. Maybe you can go catch up to the twins. I think they are out playing ball somewhere."

"Oh . . . uh . . . yeah," Wally said, heading for the door.

"But wait, Waljan!" Mrs. Pruitt grabbed his arm. "How do I look?" she asked, pinching her cheeks and straightening her hair in the mirror. Her primping for the likes of Judge Asmodeus made Wally cringe. But he made an effort to take a good look at her and give her an honest appraisal.

Wincing, Wally squinted away a painful red glare that shot into his eyes from Mrs. Pruitt's direction. Glinting in the sunshine, Asmodeus's heart-shaped ruby hung around Mrs. Pruitt's neck. This was the first time he'd noticed it. His stomach lurched, and the hair on the back of his neck began to rise.

"Well, Waljan? What do you think? I have to get the door!" she pressed.

"Uh, you look like you always do, ma'am," he answered, unnerved.

"Oh, you are no help at all! Off with you," said Mrs. Pruitt playfully, shooing him away like a fly.

Before Mrs. Pruitt reached the front door, Wally had silently slipped out the back and away. He would rather kiss a rattlesnake than play "Mr. Manners" with Asmodeus. But more importantly, he needed time away to think. The judge was plotting, that much he was sure of. He gave Mrs. Pruitt that pendant for a reason. Wally couldn't imagine Asmodeus caring for anyone, least of all Mrs. Pruitt. But it was clear to Wally that Mrs. Pruitt thought otherwise.

Nearly to the back gate, Wally stopped. A deep concern for Mrs. Pruitt took hold of him and wouldn't let go. He looked around for Tyre and Caddock, and anyone else who might be about. The yard was clear. Wally sneaked back to the house.

A laurel bush grew just below a large picture window looking into the parlor where Mrs. Pruitt entertained her visitors. Wally crouched behind it and peeked in. Asmodeus and Mrs. Pruitt sat too closely for casual acquaintances. The judge held Mrs. Pruitt's hand. Her face blushed. *So Asmodeus is Mrs. Pruitt's "gentleman"?*

Wally tried hard to make sense of their muffled conversation. Nothing. But he had seen enough.

Backing away from the window, Wally tripped over a little terra-cotta hedgehog that graced Mrs. Pruitt's flower bed and kicked the side of the wall with enough force to startle a little screech out of Mrs. Pruitt.

"Who's there?!" Asmodeus boomed. The menacing sound of angry feet followed loudly.

Wally ducked past the porch, straightened up, and sprinted to the gate. Without slowing, he hurdled over the picket fence and down the road as fast as he was able. He had to escape unseen. Cautiously ducking down alleys, through shrubberies, and under bridges, he made his way to the outskirts of town and toward Castle Wall. When he was certain that no one had followed him from the yard, he slowed to a determined walk.

Wally hopped one final creek bed before scurrying up a spongy slope. After pulling off his shoes and socks, he dropped them at the base of a gnarled tree trunk and ran his hand along Castle Wall as if greeting an old friend. Then, he plunked down on a patch of grass with a deep sigh. On previous expeditions to the wall, Wally had discovered additional breaches with falls running through, all equally treacherous and uniquely beautiful. He felt particularly drawn to this one that lay northeast of town and claimed it as his own.

What is Asmodeus up to? Wally thought, leaning back against the stony surface. He ran through all of the similarities between Mrs. Pruitt's pendant and the compass Asmodeus offered Wally. Both gifts were presented in the judge's signature box. Both were rather expensive. Both featured a heart-shaped ruby.

The strangest connection was the all-consuming misery that Wally felt in their presence. But Mrs. Pruitt didn't seem to share that experience. Thinking back on it, Wally was surprised at how unusually lighthearted she had been lately and how often—and fondly—she thought of the judge. He started to think that his imagination was crowding out his good sense. Wally's life had changed drastically, and he often felt miserably lonely for the Wood. That's expected. Perhaps it was mere coincidence that he felt it most keenly while holding Asmodeus's gifts. Nothing mysterious at all. Wally did return a very expensive necklace that the judge, a handsome and successful bachelor, wanted to give a lonely widow. Rewarding Wally would be natural. It could be all and only a matter of sentiment.

Wally's stomach growled angrily. He stood up and reached into an abandoned squirrel-hole in the gnarly tree trunk. From it, Wally pulled out a leather sack in which he'd left a chunk of dry cheese, a crusty wheat roll, and a few carrots. Gratified that no other creature had yet discovered his treasure, he plopped down on the high bank and dangled his legs above the roaring falls. The mist tickled his toes as he nibbled his carrots.

Still hungry, Wally tried the dry cheese and bread. Although tasty, they formed a lump that passed slug-like down his throat. An old canning jar from Mrs. Pruitt's kitchen hung from a length of twine tied to one of the tree's branches. Wally dipped the jar down into the rushing river and pulled up clear, cold mountain water. Relieved, refreshed, and deeply satisfied, he lay back on his mossy perch with his hands behind his head. The thundering falls lulled him into semiconsciousness.

Abruptly, a sharp pain nipped Wally's ear followed by familiar laughter. He blinked away the harsh sun rays that lined a silhouette of two figures. Caddock and Tyre snickered as Wally scrambled to his feet.

"What are you two doing here?" Wally demanded coolly, rubbing his ear where one of the boys had flicked it.

"Wondering the same thing about you," answered Caddock, glancing over at his brother with an ominous smile.

Wally turned grave. "Just leave."

"What's the matter, Lodger? Hiding something?" Caddock continued.

Wally was not in any mood to talk, least of all to these two. This was his sanctuary, a place for solitude, and now two of the people he wished to avoid most were intruding. Wally's ears grew hot and his fists clenched as he spewed his next command, "I said leave."

"And who's going to make us? You've invaded our home, Lodger. We have just as much right to your little hideaway," said Caddock. "And it's a pretty sweet spot he's got here, Tyre. I think we should build ourselves a little fort, right under this tree."

Wally could not hold back any longer. He sprang at the two and knocked them to the ground. But Caddock and Tyre were quick on their feet and soon had Wally locked in a tussle, stumbling and tripping too close to the edge of the steep bank. Tyre's footing gave way, and he arched back toward the water, pulling the other two with him. Caddock quickly dug in his heels and grabbed his brother by the collar, throwing his weight away from the water.

Reflexively, Tyre pushed off Wally to stabilize himself and launched his unfortunate lodger over the bank and into the frigid, churning waters below. Wally had just enough time to fill his lungs with air before hitting the foaming surge. He was pulled under and dragged away downriver.

"Wally!" the boys cried. They tried to catch sight of him with no luck. Caddock ran off. Tyre yelled after him, "Where are you going? We can't leave him!" But Caddock kept going as Tyre helplessly stared into the merciless torrent below him. Wally was gone.

16
Revelation

WHEN he awoke, Wally didn't understand what he saw. A warm orange glow danced before his eyes, accompanied by a quiet hissing and crackling. He focused a little harder and strange objects came into view. A fire blazed beneath a rugged, gray mantel. On the mantel, a gilded clock ticked the seconds away to the left of a polished opal stone that was twice as large as the one he found in Mrs. Pruitt's desk. Wally's arms prickled. He recalled Mrs. Pruitt's warning about the stone to "stay away from anyone who has one, uses one, talks about one" and how the stone seemed to weaken Moriel when he touched it.

Wally sat up slowly and looked around. The room was quaint. A brown wool shawl hung from a peg by a door on the wall behind him. As he puzzled out where he was and how he got there, familiarity walked through the door followed by relief. Moriel, with an armful of split logs, greeted him cheerfully.

"Well good morning, Sir Waljan! How can I be of service?" Moriel loaded the firewood into a brass bin by the fire.

"Oh, Sir Moriel! It's just you. What happened? What am I doing here?" Wally asked.

"What's the last thing you remember?" Moriel replied.

"I remember loading the candle shelf for Haden . . . and I think I am overdue on a delivery of fall bulbs to Dayton Manor."

"Well, it seems that you've lost a week of memories, son. But, that is to be expected." Moriel clapped bits of bark and dust off his hands and pulled up a small rocker. He sat. "You apparently took a tumble into the East Wall River. Either that or you decided you were a salmon and jumped in. In any case, Wally, you have been through a dangerous ordeal and are here to recuperate."

Wally pulled his legs out from under the covers one at a time. He felt weak and a little dizzy. Steadying his head with his hands, he discovered that it was wrapped in gauze.

"Now, wait just a minute," Moriel warned. "You have a concussion and a pretty nasty sprain. You need bed rest, and that foot must be elevated. Looks like you are going to be master of the house for a bit."

"Does Haden know I am here? And Mrs. Pruitt?" Wally asked.

"Of course they do. Now relax. I have some breakfast cooking out on the stove."

As soon as Moriel left the room, Wally shimmied off the bed and hopped gingerly over to the hearth, using the wall for support. He wondered why Mrs. Pruitt would be so frightened of an object that Moriel kept on his own mantel. Wally had already handled the one in her desk. The worst that happened was her reaction. Still, remembering her fear set him on edge.

Wally extended a single finger toward the stone. The object brightened. Flinching, he drew his hand quickly away. The light waned. Come on, Wally, relax. It's not going to detonate! he thought to himself. Again, he brought his hand over the stone. It radiated an intense, bluish light and began to sing in high tones like the lip of a crystal glass when rubbed with moist fingers. The sound grew. "Shhhhh!" Wally insisted, pulling his hand away. But the pads of his fingertips nicked the stone's surface. The stone spun off the hearth, upsetting the iron fireplace tools and sending them crashing to the ground with unfortunate force.

Moriel burst through the door. "Wally! Are you . . ."

Wally limped back to bed like Bo Dog after shredding Haden's leather slippers.

Moriel straightened up the tools and retrieved the stone that had rolled to the other side of the room. As if carrying an injured bird, he cradled the stone and returned it to its perch. Then he lowered himself on one knee, paused, and rose.

Turning to Wally he said, "Sneaking won't do here. You simply have to ask. I can understand you have concerns about that stone. But trust me. Mrs. Pruitt's fear is misplaced. That is all you need to know for now."

"Yes, sir," Wally replied.

"I will be right back with your food. Please. Stay in the bed. Touch nothing."

Breakfast cured much of Wally's lightheadedness, and he was ready to get out of bed. But Moriel insisted he stay put.

Moriel cleared away the dishes and took a seat at the end of the cot. "I need to ask you something," he said.

Wally felt a little uneasy at this.

"What on earth were you doing back at a Wall breach? I hear that you have made the trip repeatedly. Haden has warned you about how dangerous those falls can be."

Wally was perplexed. He thought no one knew about his private getaway by the falls. But having lost a few days of his memory, he had to assume that Moriel wasn't simply guessing. "I don't know, Sir Moriel. I just have to be there. I feel settled. Safe. Home. And nothing I've been told about it makes sense."

"And what is sensible about falling in a river? The force of water careening down that mountain is enough to knock down a forest of trees. It could tear you apart."

"I just mean that the world doesn't end at the Wall," said Wally. "Something's got to be there. I just know it. Whatever it is, I just feel like I am part of it."

"I see. Well . . ." Moriel leaned in on his elbows and clasped his hands against his chin. "I guess you are ready to hear the full truth. There is something there. You asked me when we first met whether there was a castle beyond the wall."

"I was right! I knew it! So the stories I heard as a child, the stories about the King of the Realm . . . they're all true?" Wally asked, wide-eyed.

"Yes, they are," Moriel answered.

"But if no one has traveled beyond the wall and returned, how do you know?" Wally asked.

"I know because I have met the one who lives there."

Wally's pulse quickened.

Moriel continued, "I am a Knight of Abidan, the Realm of Mist and Mercy. I serve the King."

Now remembering his first introduction, Wally said quietly to himself, "Moriel of the Realm." He nearly jumped out of his bed, but feeling the ache in his head and ankle more keenly now, he contained his excitement.

"Can I meet him? Can you take me to him?" Wally pleaded.

"I intend to, Wally," replied Moriel. "I believe the King has a particular plan for you."

"How is that even possible? The King doesn't know me."

"You don't know him. But that doesn't mean he doesn't know you. The King is very powerful. His presence is everywhere felt. He has ways of watching, of knowing. Those destined for knighthood are drawn to the kingdom like a seedling is drawn to the sun."

"Destined for knighthood? Me?" Wally asked, humbled at the suggestion.

"That may explain your interest in Castle Wall, having no other knowledge or experience of the King."

"Why hasn't Haden mentioned this to me before?"

"There are many reasons, some that shouldn't surprise you. Haden is not exactly the best communicator, wouldn't you agree? We in the kingdom are each given different gifts. We fill different roles. I could not serve as I do without Haden's friendship and support. But he is more comfortable with objects than ideas."

"He's admitted as much," Wally recalled. "What happens now?"

"We look for certain qualities in a knight. We couldn't be certain of your potential without time, study, and training. And we can't proceed unless you desire it."

"Desire it? Who wouldn't want to be a knight, Moriel!"

"Well, now, Wally, hold on. Knighthood is not what you hear about in storybooks. It is not glory in battle and riches and pretty girls swooning over your heroism. It takes discipline, hard work, and sacrifice. And it can be very lonely."

Wally considered Moriel's words for a moment. "Sir, I know of only one knight. He is kind. He is strong. He is wise. If being a knight means I might become more like him, I am ready to begin."

17
First Things First

IT wasn't what he expected. He could take discipline, hard work, and sacrifice. And he knew what it was like to be lonely. But whatever being a knight involved, it couldn't have much to do with books. Or so Wally thought.

With his foot resting on a pile of pillows, Wally studied the Edicts of the Eternal Realm. Mrs. Pruitt had proven herself a worthy teacher, and he resented it. He didn't want to read his way to knighthood. Restless from hours of slogging through material he barely understood, Wally closed the book and set it on the side table. He grabbed the crutches that Moriel made for him and hobbled out into the sunshine.

"Finished so soon?" Moriel asked as he tended his herbs.

"Did you expect me to be?"

"No. But you're out here."

"Oh, Moriel, come on! Really? I can't just sit all day; let me help you."

"You can't do much more than sit, Waljan. You need to keep that leg up. But I suppose some fresh air would do you good. Go sit up against that tree stump."

As Wally nestled in against the stump, Moriel bunched up a length of burlap and tucked it under Wally's injured leg.

"So, do you have any questions from your reading?" Moriel asked as he freed the rose bushes from a prison of weeds.

"No. I mean, yeah. I mean, oh, there's just too much I don't understand. It's hard to get through. I do have questions about the King, though."

"Really?" Moriel asked, glancing over his shoulder as he worked in the soil.

"I've never met a king. I don't know how to greet him . . . or what to say. Do I bow? Or kneel? You have to be careful about that stuff. I heard one story where a soldier forgot to lower his eyes in front of a king, and he was blinded and then thrown into a pit!"

"Hmm. Does seem harsh, doesn't it," said Moriel.

"It would be hard not to look at him," Wally continued. "But the King of the Realm must not look like a king. You've seen him, Moriel. Does he look like a king, or does he just blend in with everyone else? If he blended in that would explain why I have never seen him before even though . . ."

Moriel straightened up and turned. "Now hold on, Wally, first things first. Your many questions can be answered by reading a book you refuse to finish."

"I didn't say I wouldn't finish. It's just hard."

"I know. But you have time," Moriel replied. "You will never meet the King if you don't first understand his ways. The Edicts help us to learn them. In the Realm, the Abidan people know the Edicts so well that obeying them becomes part of their very nature. Anyone who desires to live with them has to know the Edicts just as well."

"Is he actually making you read the Edicts, Boy?" a voice, followed by joyful baying, echoed up from the path approaching Moriel's hut.

"Haden! Bo Dog!" Wally shouted, trying to get to his feet. Moriel put a hand on his shoulder, keeping him down.

"No, no, Wally, don't get up for me," Haden laughed.

Bo Dog flew over the lawn and pounced on his vulnerable master, panting, wriggling, and wagging.

"Now, Haden, don't start making my job harder by siding with Wally over reading the Edicts! You know he's got a lot to learn if he wants to join the community."

"That's right, you'll be joining us for the next Gathering I hear."

"I hope so, Sir," Wally said.

"I thought you might need a couple things to help you recover in comfort. Cullie brought these over for you on the last wagon." Haden handed Wally his bow and quiver and a picture of Penelope fishing in Meander Creek.

"Where did you get this?" Wally asked.

"Well, apparently Culbert has a bit of his dad's art talent. He drew that picture of Peep himself, just the other day. Now check those arrows, and the tension on your bow. It probably needs maintenance."

"Yes, Sir," Wally said dutifully and then turned his attention to Bo's upturned belly.

Haden grabbed Moriel's arm and moved him out of Wally's earshot. "We've got trouble in town. Things are really getting out of hand, and people are starting to take sides. Neighbors who once got along are now making accusations against one another. I had to break up a heated argument between Josiah and one of his best customers. This is not like him, Moriel. He is starting to see everyone who comes into the store as a thief, obsessed with being a victim. With the increase in crime, he sees Malvo and his boys as a necessary evil."

"'Necessary evil' is right. They enforce the laws they break. Malvo is both criminal and lawman. We have only seen these incidents go up since these men arrived in town," Moriel confided in hushed tones.

"I was thinking the same thing. But we have even bigger problems. The council is moving to outlaw all Abidanian literature as treasonous. They are afraid that the increase in devotion to the King will undermine the city leadership."

"Yes, Gerald Guest's customers have already been harassed over that. Okay. Let's get the elders together at Geezer's. We can use the banquet room on the second floor. I planned on coming into town tomorrow. We can meet then."

* * * * *

Chatter and footfalls echoed through the emptied space as the Abidanians of Mortinburg crowded into the Geyser's banquet room to meet with Moriel and The Twelve. Haden and Chaz Myrtle, a successful rancher who had known Haden for many years, came early to help Geez set up. Wooden benches replaced the overstuffed red velvet chairs and the dining tables were stacked against a hallway wall. Still, there was little room even for those who chose to stand. Everyone worried about the growing persecution against the King and its impact on their own lives.

Moriel addressed the assembly on behalf of The Twelve, the elders who, like Moriel, had achieved knighthood. "Asmodeus and his men create fear and then use it to control how people think and what they do. If we stay loyal to the King, we have nothing to fear. And then he has no control over us."

Chaz Myrtle responded, "It is only a matter of time before someone gets hurt. I don't think the Sweets Shop attack was a random incident by rowdy troublemakers."

"What do you mean, Chaz?" Moriel asked.

"Polly Sweet can tell you. She's here somewhere."

A short, round woman with pink skin and spectacles spoke up. "Yes, I'm here. A week before the attack on the shop I was experimenting with something I called a Crown Cake. It was a beautiful little muffin shaped like a king's crown with little jewels made out of colored hard candies. They were quite delicious with golden cake on the inside—I used golden cake of course because . . ."

Chaz cut her off. "Polly, dear, we're certain they were wonderful, but if you would get to the part about the attack, it would be very helpful."

"Oh yes, I'm sorry. Well, Officer Krass and Officer Bader came in for some chocolate covered coffee beans. That was their favorite, you know. And Officer Krass wanted to try a Crown Cake. He agreed that they were quite stunning. Well, I was delighted! But the other officer, Bader, he seemed to think that the cakes undermined the social order. I'm not even sure what that means. Anyway, he told me I had to throw them all away!

"Well, I had worked hard on those cakes and I told him I didn't appreciate his opinion. He was very cross with me after that. Officer Krass sneaked by the next morning and bought one from me anyway." Polly Sweet smiled triumphantly. And then, a melancholy came over her. "And then they came. Those men wearing masks. And they smashed my windows and threw my displays to the ground and…". Polly couldn't finish. She sat down.

"And we all know about what happened to Gerald Guest at the hands of Bruce Malvo," someone yelled from the crowd.

Raziel Keeper, of the Mortinburg Library and History Museum added, "I have had written threats against the library for all Abidanian literature: histories, diaries, poetry, fiction. I've had to pull them off the shelves and store them for safety."

The chief elder, Sir Allred, calmed the uproar that followed. "We all know that Mortania has been ruled through the ages by the House of Uriel and that his line is hostile to the King of the Realm. And though we've enjoyed a period of relative peace recently, make no mistake. We are at war, my friends. Miss Sweet's is just one of many incidents we can cite. As long as Abidan remains unknown, the Enemy has no reason to fight. But, as we increase, so does his need to fight back. We must remain loyal to the King to the end.

"That being said, I think it is wise for us to be more cautious about our words and actions when it comes to the city. There is no reason for us to poke at the wasps' nest, agreed? And let's encourage one another. Brother Haden, please start a collection for Miss Sweet."

After the collection was taken up, all present recited the Abidanian Loyalty Oath. Then, Sir Allred adjourned the meeting.

When Moriel returned from town, he found Wally beating the dust out of an area rug with one of his crutches. Bo Dog lay nearby, happily working on a steer bone.

"Well, look at you!" Moriel said in surprise. "Do you think you can get along without those crutches now?"

"Not until the rugs are clean, anyway," Wally joked.

"Sit down and let me take a look," Moriel said. He knelt down and set Wally's weak ankle up on his knees. Pressing, prodding, and twisting gently, he decided that Wally would be walking easily by the time of the Gathering. "Healing nicely, but I still want you to stay off of it. It is very easy to reinjure a weak ankle."

Moriel reached out to pet Bo as the dog scraped the meat away from his bone.

Bo snapped at Moriel's hand and growled a low warning.

"Whoa! This dog has an attitude, Wally. Are you sure he's safe?"

Wally reached down calmly and pulled the bone away from Bo who wagged his tail and whined in protest. Then Wally handed it back. "He just needs to know you. That's all."

"Well, I hope we get to know each other soon then!" Moriel said. "Come in the house. I brought you something from town."

Moriel dropped a package on the table and unwrapped it. "Turn around." He held a pale green linen tunic across Wally's shoulders. "That will do just fine I think. Here, try these on. It's not appropriate to enter the presence of the King in shabby work clothes."

Wally donned his new clothes and limped out to the retention pond to check his reflection. Flourishes in emerald and sapphire thread traveled along the neckline and down the center of the tunic that hung loosely over suede trousers. Soft moccasins with polished glass clasps covered his feet. Wally dashed back in as quickly as his crutches would carry him.

"I don't know what to say, Moriel."

"Well, you can thank our seamstress Rachel at the Gathering. She makes many of the garments for our celebrations." Moriel looked Waljan over, circling him. "You look very fine, Wally. And now, we have a few more things to go over before you are ready. The Gathering is a sacred event. Do you know what that means?"

Wally shook his head.

"It is the quality that inspires a person to be very still and quiet, to hold on to a moment as if it were a precious stone. It is much like sighting a majestic buck on an early morning walk, or witnessing an eclipse of the moon. The Misting Chamber, where we gather, is a solemn place. It is a place to think and watch, a place of respect. Do you understand?"

"I think so, sir," Wally replied. "Penelope—she is the girl in the picture Haden brought me—she once spooked a stag that I was hunting. She said that she'd been watching him and that he was too beautiful to shoot. Is that what you mean?"

"To a degree, yes," Moriel said. "There is one more thing you must know. The Gathering meets secretly. There are forces in Mortania who are threatened by those they don't understand."

"Malvo and his gang."

"Yes, Wally. And Asmodeus. Some who are given authority over others guard their power jealously. They believe I represent a rival. And in a way, I do. Until we are well represented among the leadership of our cities, Abidanians are in danger. Many of them work and live in Mortinburg. No matter what, you are not to breathe a word about the Gathering to anyone or reveal the identity of those attending."

18
In the Courtyard

WALLY fastened the toggles on his tunic and pulled his golden locks into a tail at the back of his neck. He took care to present himself at his best; he even cleaned his fingernails. After nestling his feet into his new moccasins, Wally grabbed his bow and quill. Just outside the hut door, Moriel waited, dressed in regalia Wally had never seen.

"Wow, Moriel. You look amazing. No one would mess with you looking like that!"

Instead of his typical brown habit and sandals, animal skin boots covered his lower legs, met by a pleated tunic of deep purple wool. The tunic was gathered at the waist by a thick band of black leather over which the tails of a thick leather vest fell. From his belt hung Paraclete. Many folds of cape in black wool clasped at his neck and draped down Moriel's back, and a small circlet crown rested on his head. He was a magnificent sight. Wally could not take his eyes off of him.

"Well, my young page, are we going to stand here gawking at one another, or should we be on our way? Don't want to be late for your first Gathering!" Moriel prodded.

The two set out on foot, accompanied by silver moonlight. For a time they walked silently, but after the chirping of crickets and the wild noises of the night no longer held their attention, Wally couldn't help but ask more questions.

"Are there any Abidanians my age at the Gathering?"

"Of course," Moriel said. "People of all ages serve the King."

"Are they all knights?"

"Well, is Haden a knight? No. There are many ways to serve."

"Haden will be at the Gathering tonight, right?" Wally asked.

"He wouldn't miss it."

The pair walked on awhile before Wally drummed up the courage to ask, "Moriel, have you ever used your sword in a real battle?"

"A 'real' battle? You mean against a whole army rather than four cowards with a whip?"

"Yeah," Wally said enthusiastically.

Moriel looked off in the distance. "Wally, it is something I dread. Every soul is precious to the King. War isn't glorious or exciting. It is grave. It is mournful. Sometimes it is necessary. But it isn't something I want to talk much about."

The questions ended, and they continued on in silence until they finally reached the Eastern Ridge Falls. With Castle Wall on their left, the two descended a small hidden pathway toward the falls and made a sharp turn. There, before crossing through an opening in the Wall, Moriel whispered to Wally to remove his moccasins and leave them at the base of a large cedar tree. They slipped through the narrow opening, and then Wally realized where he was. His chest fluttered and little bumps raised up on his arms.

"Moriel! . . ." Wally's voice echoed down the granite tunnel despite the hushing thrum of water. Moriel brought a finger to his lips and shook his head. This was the time for reflection, not speech.

"But Moriel!" Wally continued softly and eagerly, "We've crossed under the Wall! We are in Abidan!"

Moriel whispered, "If Abidan were a mansion, we would be in the courtyard, so yes, in a way, we are."

Under Wally's feet, cool sand cushioned his steps, and the air, freshened by the falls, streamed in through portals above. Dancing yellow torchlight traveled over the blue moonlit walls. As they followed the bends and dips, the soothing warmth of human voices singing in unison reached Wally's ears.

Presently, the tunnel opened to a large but intimate grotto full of people. Some Wally recognized. Haden approached, embraced Moriel, and tousled Wally's hair playfully. Others followed to greet the two.

Moriel broke away and brought Wally forward. In the center of the room a subterranean pool reflected the moonlight in all directions leaving pale streaks swimming like schooling fish about the ceiling and walls. It was uniquely beautiful. Moriel stooped down and carefully washed his face and hands in the water, directing Wally to do the same.

On the other side of the pool, a rocky platform rose. There, a man the people called Sir Idan prepared to speak. Everyone settled on the sandy floor, and he began.

"Long ago, before memory, the Kingdom of the Eternal Realm, Abidan, extended as far as the eye could see. From Castle Mount it ran in all directions, into the foothills, over the plains, and all the way to the great oceans, where no one had ever traveled. There was no divide between the land and its Ruler. Light streamed from the castle and warmed the land. Fed by the mystical waters of the castle moat, rivers gracefully flowed over the plains that provided rich food for the people.

"The King enjoyed his people, walking among them, eating with them, calling them his friends. But the King's advisers thought it wrong for royalty to mix with commoners. Uriel, the Chief Adviser to the King, grew jealous of the King's love for his people. And that jealousy turned into resentment and then hatred. Uriel traveled into the land and spread rumors about the King. The people began to question why the King should dwell in the Castle of Light while his subjects had to be content in the valleys below. They started to wonder why they could not rule themselves. Soon, anger and distrust spread among them, and the beautiful land of the Eternal Realm became a miserable land of anger, war, and evil. Saddened by their betrayal, the King erected a wall and shut them out of the Kingdom.

"So, Uriel led the people in revolt. They made plans to breach the wall and overthrow the King. They would not succeed. No one but the King himself can break down the walls of Abidan. But there was no need.

"Knowing Uriel's desire for war, the King and his knights came down from Castle Mount to meet Uriel's army. He dismounted Regal, his pure white stallion, withdrew his sword from its sheath, and handed it to his general. Unarmed, he approached his wayward people.

"Removing his crown, the King addressed Uriel, 'You are now the king of this land.' He then raised his voice for all to hear. 'This land shall now be known as Mortania, the land of death. Those who choose life, choose Abidan and must follow me beyond the wall. I will wait for you.' And he dropped the crown at Uriel's feet. The people did not understand. They grew angry and violent. To the astonishment of all, the King refused to defend himself. He held out his arms to each side as if accepting whatever fate the people chose. Some knew then that the King was innocent of Uriel's accusations. But the evil hoards attacked their unarmed King, and he was no more."

Every person in the room lowered their head and remained silent as if time had stopped. Wally could hardly breathe. But . . . the King is dead? How can the King be dead? Wally thought. When the crowd raised their heads the speaker continued.

"But death has no place in the Eternal Realm. Death exists only in Mortania. So through death, the King climbed Castle Wall and returned to his Kingdom, where he awaits the return of his people."

Now, everyone stood and began to sing a tune that Wally had heard before, on the first day he had seen Castle Wall.

The bards are mute, the songs unsung
But you are not forgotten.
The waters hum, "Dear children, come,
The King waits in the mist!"
So, gather in, our joys begin
The King waits in the mist!"

As they sang, a mist gathered above the pool from all about the cavern and settled there. Whispers could be heard declaring, "The King arrives!" and people filed toward the pool. The music continued.

Not all who see have noticed Thee
Nor those who hear detect You near.

The blind perceive, the deaf believe,
The King waits in the mist!
So, gather in, our joys begin
The King waits in the mist!

Our Regent wise, no good you spare
The children of your Kingdom fair
But should we stray, and turn away
The King waits in the mist.
His mercy's deep and Love will keep;
He's waiting in the mist.

So when the pain of life has stained
Your heart coal black, the world disdained
No plight too grim, return to him,
The King waits in the mist!
So gather in, too long it's been;
The King waits in the mist!

As each person approached the mist in turn, they knelt briefly and then waded into the pool. Stopping in the center, they extended their arms, just as the King had done before Uriel in the story. After a short time they folded their hands before them and proceeded out of the pool and into an after chamber.

Wally saw Haden approach the water and got up to follow, but Moriel stopped him. "Wally, stay away from the pool. It is not for those who are not yet prepared."

"But this is what we have been studying for," Wally replied. "I am prepared."

"I know you believe that. But tell me, son. Look hard. Do you see the King?" Moriel asked.

Wally looked around the room, perplexed.

"No, Wally, in the mist. Can you see him?" Moriel repeated.

"There's nothing there but mist. I don't know what you mean," Wally replied.

"Exactly," Moriel said. "The mist is sacred. It requires that you fully understand and appreciate what you encounter there. It would be dangerous to approach it casually. You can meet the others in the after chamber. There is a back door behind us. Go and I will be there shortly."

Suddenly, Wally felt oddly out of place. He thought he was called to be a knight of the Realm. All he knew now was that the King was dead, and, after weeks of preparation for this meeting, he was still unprepared. He wondered what he was doing here.

Bewildered, Wally caught up with Haden, who began to introduce him to those he'd never met. Wally already knew many there. These people with whom he had lived from day to day in Mortinburg—merchants, farmers, craftsmen, and healers—now took on a new role. They welcomed him warmly and the uneasiness left him.

"So, Waljan, what did you think of your first Gathering?" asked Chaz Myrtle.

Wally answered, "I don't know. I'm confused. I thought I was preparing to meet the King. I'm not sure what I am doing here."

Everyone shot knowing glances at one another, making Wally feel like he was the subject of a joke he didn't understand.

"Only you can say what you are doing here, Waljan," said Chaz. "But we understand why you would be confused. What did you think of our story?"

"It didn't make any sense to me. Why would a powerful king, with a trained army, meet a traitor and his civilian troops in battle only to surrender? He had the force. He had the right!"

"It was an illusion, really," Chaz explained. "Uriel had divided the kingdom in two. The true kingdom, Abidan, belongs to the one true King. It is an everlasting kingdom of peace, love, and joy. The very source of life in the world flows through Abidan. Its waters sustain us even now. The land that we live in was once a part of Abidan. But when Uriel claimed it as his own, he cut it off from the source of its life. It became Mortania, the kingdom of death, a land that must one day come to an end. The King only surrendered what had already been lost. But Uriel did not understand this. He believed that by ruling Mortania he would rule the King of Abidan as well. He was very wrong."

Wally objected, "But he did not just surrender the land. He surrendered himself. Why didn't he allow his army to defend him?"

Sir Idan Teller, who presided over the meeting, overheard Wally's questions and joined the conversation. "Because he wanted the people to understand how much he loved them and wanted to be reunited to them. He knew that by choosing to lose everything for their sake, and even to die for them, some would come to understand his goodness and truth, and follow him back to Abidan."

"But he died! How can they follow him if he is dead?" Wally asked.

Idan turned to Moriel. "So, this is the boy you have been telling me about?"

"Yes, he is."

Idan continued, "And yet he lives. He died in the land of death. But death has no power in Abidan. The few Mortanians who remained loyal to the King returned his body to this very cavern and placed it at the edge of the Misting Pool. The pool is a passage to the Eternal Realm. It is here that the King awakened and passed on to Abidan. It is here that he returns to meet with those who long to join him."

"So he's alive? Is that why you asked me if I can see him in the mist, Moriel?"

"Yes, Wally."

Then Wally asked Ida, "What happens to those who don't return to Abidan?"

"The King cannot demand what must be freely given. Those who choose not to return will never climb Castle Wall. They will die in Mortania and die with Mortania. It is not his desire. But, it wouldn't be love if it were taken by force."

The deep love that the King showed for his people awed Wally into silence. He could ask no more questions.

19
Hunting Crows

WITH a crack and a thump, Wally's ax head stuck fast in a stump, sending two halves of firewood to the ground. Moriel stacked the wood as Wally wriggled the ax free. Completely healed, Wally had returned to Mrs. Pruitt's home. But he still spent his afternoons with Moriel, preparing for knighthood. This was a welcome change, even when lessons accompanied chores.

"I still don't understand why people don't return to Abidan the normal way one returns to a place," Wally said.

"And what way is that, Wally?" Moriel said.

"I don't know. By just going there. Abidan is right there on the other side of the wall. There must be some way around. It's just a wall."

"Is it?" Moriel replied. "Just a wall? It's the King's wall. How do you think a king would react if trespassers invaded his territory?" He tossed a few logs on the wood pile and sat down to rest.

"They wouldn't be trespassing. Sir Ida said that the King invited anyone who desired to return. If only we could see what lies beyond the wall, if we could all see the kingdom and the King, maybe more people would," Wally argued.

"Those who are invited come through a gate, Wally. Those who trespass sneak over a wall."

"But there is no gate, Moriel. What are we supposed to do? Fly through the mist?"

Moriel took a swig of water from a large wooden cup and wiped his forehead on his sleeve. Then, he picked up his wedge and mallet and returned to his work.

"How did the King himself travel from Mortania to Abidan?"

"He died," Wally said.

"Exactly. We wait for the King's timing. Don't start thinking like Uriel, as if you know better than the King himself. All you need to do is serve him. Asmodeus has a way of telling the truth to suit his own purposes. And he and his men are right to a point. There is a black abyss on the other side of the wall waiting for those who attempt to reach Abidan their own way. If Asmodeus knew how much you wanted to scale that wall, he would have given you some rope by now. The only way that leads safely to Abidan is the King's way."

Furrowing his brow, Wally held the ax close against his chest. With a toss of his head he directed Moriel's attention to several men approaching.

"As if our words were the wind, Wally, here comes the storm," Moriel said.

Asmodeus's thugs, Malvo, Coleman, Krass, and Bader, sauntered up the lawn, taking stock of the surroundings. From inside the hut, Bo Dog started to bark ferociously.

"Nice setup you have here, Moriel," Malvo said. "Or should I call you 'sir' or something? Maybe I should bow?"

The men laughed.

"Can I help you with something?" Moriel asked.

"There's been some talk in town. The judge would like to see you. He's . . . er . . . worried about you," said Malvo, followed by more snickering from his men.

"Oh, he needn't worry, boys. I can take care of myself. But I expect you know that."

The men fell silent.

"Well, we have orders to bring you in. Now. Official business," Malvo replied. "And you need to leave that frog sticker of yours here. You are coming with us unarmed."

"I see. Well, if you put it that way, how could I refuse? But first, I need to give young Wally some chores to do while I am gone. Do you mind?"

The men allowed Moriel to take Wally around to the shed. When he knew they were out of earshot, Moriel said, "Asmodeus is going to ask me questions about our Gatherings. I need to give you an important task."

"Moriel, you can't go with those men!" Wally pleaded. "Not without your sword."

"You don't need to be concerned, son."

"But Asmodeus is up to something we don't understand. I haven't brought this up to you because I really wasn't sure whether I was making a lot out of nothing. But, this is not just about city business, Moriel. The judge has a mysterious way of controlling people. He gave Mrs. Pruitt a necklace. I didn't really notice it before, but now that I think back, it made her personality change. She was more . . . well, girly."

Moriel raised his eyebrows and suppressed a chuckle. "Girly? Isn't that what happens when women receive gifts?"

"No, really, Moriel. You have to believe me! He tried to give me something, too—a compass with a ruby inside, just like Mrs.

Pruitt's necklace, but smaller. Both times I held one of these rubies my feelings changed instantly. And Mr. Constance . . . I heard you talking to Haden about how afraid he's been and I've been thinking. Mr. Constance has a key chain with all kinds of gems and charms on it!"

"Okay, okay. Calm down. We can talk about this later. But right now I have to get back to Malvo. Don't worry about Asmodeus. He has more to fear from me than I from him. That is why I need your help. I need you and Bo to keep Paraclete well hidden. There is a loose panel by the bed for that purpose. You must stay here and guard it until I return. Do you understand?"

"But what if you need it in town?"

"I'll be all right. I can't risk bringing Paraclete into a meeting with Asmodeus. It will only cause trouble. Don't be afraid. I will be back here in the morning."

"Yes, sir," Wally responded.

The men surrounded Moriel and escorted him off into the woods. As soon as they were out of sight of the hut, Malvo pulled a long blade from his boot and flashed it in Moriel's face.

"No one makes a fool out of me in front of the entire town!" he sneered.

"No one has to. You do pretty well without their help," Moriel teased.

"You think you are courageous," Malvo replied as Bader started to tie Moriel's hands behind his back and Coleman covered his eyes with a sack.

"Well, that depends on whom I compare myself to. Here I am, weaponless, outnumbered, and you're tying my hands. Why didn't you tie me up at the hut? Afraid a scrawny kid and his puppy were going to stop you?"

"Keep quiet!" Malvo screamed. "You can make jokes from the bottom of the river. Let's go!"

The men grabbed Moriel by his arms and ran him down the forested hill, through the brush. With his eyes covered, he couldn't keep his footing well and fell more than once. Malvo barked out commands, and the men grunted out responses, making it very difficult for Moriel to listen for clues as to where he was. Then they all came to a hard stop. Moriel could then make out the sound of rushing water, straight ahead.

"What was that, boss?" said Coleman.

"I dunno. I can't hear nothin' but the river in the canyon."

Everyone tried to calm their breathing and listen closer. A puff of air batted the sack that covered Moriel's face, followed by a thud and then a horrible wail from Bruce Malvo. "I've been hit!" Then another thud landed above the men's heads.

"Run!" Coleman shrieked.

Chaos erupted with snaps and cracks, the rustling of branches, and the knocking of loosened stones.

"Don't go that way, you fools!" Moriel heard Malvo yelling, then two cries and moments later the splash of water breaking.

Calm finally returned and Moriel stood alone. Footsteps came downhill and the sack that covered Moriel popped off. Wally stood in front of him, smiling, with his bow and quill slung over his shoulder.

"Wally! What are you doing?"

"Untying you," Wally said as he worked the ropes apart.

"But I told you to stay home and protect my sword!"

"Paraclete is very well protected, trust me," Wally said, searching for the arrow that he'd seen Malvo pull from his arm.

Moriel puzzled out the possibilities. "Haden?"

"Nope. Bo Dog." The arrow caught Wally's eye. "There it is!"

"Wally! How do you expect a dog to protect my sword?"

"You'll see."

Moriel and Wally returned to the hut.

"Where is it?" Moriel demanded, anxiously.

"Under the floor board by the bed, like you asked."

Moriel entered the hut. There was Bo Dog, lying on top of the loose board, working through a very large, meaty thigh bone.

"I dare you to get him away from that door," Wally laughed.

20
The Spirit Sword

IT didn't take long for news to spread that the bodies of officers Jahn Krass and Bach Bader had been found by the fishing dock after washing downstream. That Bruce Malvo showed up to work with a deep shoulder wound the same day made everyone in town suspicious and speculative. Coleman claimed that he got careless with a whittling knife, and neither man had any comment on their comrades' demise. But since the men were already the subject of much argument in town, these events only brought the discussion from a simmer to a full boil.

Having returned to work at the Mercantile on limited hours following his accident, Wally spent just enough time in town to pick up on all the talk. As he swept out from under the feed bins before opening one morning, he heard a thump at the front display window. Wally leaned the broom against the wall and hauled the trash basket to the back door. Then, he went to check the front. On the outside of the display window someone had posted a notice, signed by Bruno Daggot, Mayor of Mortinburg:

Notice of City Ordinance
Effective Immediately
By the Office of City Management

The Office of City Management hereby declares that
in light of the tragic deaths of Mortinburg enforcement officers
Krass and Bader, all speech construed to criticize, undermine,
subvert, or otherwise interfere with city
business shall hereby be subject to a fine, incarceration,
or both pending investigation by the Office of Enforcement.

After his shift, Wally brought the notice to Moriel, who had stayed close to home until the commotion in town died down. Moriel took one look at the notice and threw it into the fire pit.

"Come with me, Wally," he said.

Wally followed Moriel down a heavily wooded trail that opened into an arena. Burlap bags stuffed with straw sat atop wooden poles around the arena, along with a number of obstacles and targets designed to improve a warrior's agility, strength, and aim.

Wally welled up in excitement. "Do I start my training today?"

"I have word that two Abidanians were arrested in town yesterday, and now this ridiculous ordinance," Moriel said. "I am afraid we need to be ready to defend ourselves, the community, and, most importantly, the King. He is counting on us to lead his people back to him. We can't do that from a jail cell. So yes, training starts today.

"You are very handy with your bow, as I have been fortunate to know firsthand. But a Knight of the Realm is equipped with very special weapons." Moriel directed Wally to a table at the center of the arena where a lonely bundle wrapped in linen lay. "Open it carefully," he said.

As Wally gently spread the edges of the linen aside, a silver gleam met his eyes. A steel, double-edged blade reflected back his own stunned expression. Polished gems of brilliant hues studded the most beautiful hilt Wally had ever seen.

He backed away. "Sir Moriel, you can't be giving this to me!"

"Go ahead, Wally, pick it up," Moriel said with a sparkle in his eye.

Wally approached the sword and slipped his fingers around the hilt. He tried to lift the weapon, but it wouldn't move. Using both hands, he yanked with all his strength, but it stuck fast as if bolted down. He even tried to slide the blade toward him. It simply wouldn't budge.

"It doesn't fit me, Moriel," Wally complained. "It is entirely too heavy!"

"On the contrary, Wally," Moriel responded, "You don't fit the sword. This is a Spirit Sword of the Eternal Realm. When you have proven yourself loyal to the King, you will find it quite easy to wield."

"But how am I going to learn to fight and prove myself if I can't lift the sword?" Wally asked.

"Oh, you don't prove yourself by fighting, Wally. That is a certain way to die. You prove yourself through love and discipline. Only those who have proven themselves are strong enough to wear the armor and to fight for the King. And even then, a knight is only effective if he is united with the King. It is the King's strength that wins the knight's battle. We are just the instrument through which he does it. That is why we gather and meet him in the mist. We gain strength for the battle from the King himself."

"What do I do then?" Wally asked.

Moriel explained. "First, you must dedicate yourself to the Truth. Never be false. Wear Truth like a belt around your waist. Next, you must desire above all to promote the good and reject evil. Let your heart deflect evil like a breastplate deflects a blow. Third, as sturdy shoes prepare your feet for a journey, prepare yourself to carry the news of the King to all you meet. Sacrifice yourself for the good of others, just as the King sacrificed himself for the people. And, finally, trust in the King's love. His servants will shield you from those who want you to fail."

"Like Asmodeus," Wally said.

"For one," Moriel replied. "But there are others. The House of Uriel still rules Mortania. No one realizes that Uriel continues to rule because he does so quietly. Secretly. Strategically. Just as the King has his knights, Uriel has many who serve him. Asmodeus serves him. Uriel is cunning and very dangerous. He would just as soon steal your hopes of returning to Abidan as look at you. But the King is with you. And his promise of life will protect you as certain as a battle helmet."

Claiming the Spirit Sword as his own became Wally's single desire. It meant that the King found Wally worthy of Knighthood. Before he could claim it, he had to be able to lift it.

With Bader and Krass gone, and the Abidanians' caution around town, the citizens settled back into a tense calm with fewer incidents of violence and crime. Moriel had more time to work with Wally. The months marched into fall. Wally studied, worked, trained, and spent a lot of time with the Abidanians. Each time he attended the Gathering, he learned a bit more of the history of Abidan and the ways of the King. Through the winter, he grew taller and stronger.

Even when he wasn't training or spending time with the community of Abidanians, Wally found himself feeling more connected to everything. He smiled more. He bought groceries for Mrs. Pruitt on the way home from the Mercantile and performed odd jobs around the house as needed. He randomly offered assistance to an overburdened worker, a lost child, a dog tangled in its leash.

All the while, the town buzzed with anticipation of the Centennial Jubilee, celebrating the installation of the clock tower a hundred years before. Planning had occupied the town leaders for many months, and as the event approached, the citizens of Mortinburg seemed to forget their disagreements and turned their thoughts to the celebration. The Mercantile swarmed with customers and shipments. Wally worked diligently, often at chores he wasn't assigned, just to be helpful at this especially busy time. Mr. Constance was so impressed with Wally's effort that he increased his pay.

Wally even tried to befriend old Allie. But to his utter confusion, the more he tried, the more aloof she became. Now she preferred to observe him from afar. So he left her little gifts instead. He would use his earnings to buy food, or practical little items like sweet smelling soap, or a brush for her wild hair. Once he bought her a soft, warm shawl that she could wrap herself up in at night.

As he met up with Haden one evening on their way to the Gathering, he caught a glimpse of Allie in a dirty corner under the Mercantile walkway. She huddled with the shawl wrapped tightly around her, rocking herself back and forth and weeping.

"Haden, what do you know about Allie?"

"Not much, why?"

"I don't know. I just wonder how she got to this point. How did she wind up so alone?"

"She's been this way as long as I have known of her, Wally. People say she's crazy."

"Maybe she's just lost. I was lost once. What would have happened to me had you not come along?"

"Well I did come along, Waljan. You don't need to worry."

"I'm not worried. I just wish someone could do the same for her."

"So you have found some compassion for the 'old hag' as you once called her?" Haden said with a warm smile. "That's good. Seeing things from the top down."

"I suppose," Wally said.

"So now, how about the Pruitt twins? Any closer to forging a friendship there?" Haden asked.

"I haven't seen much of them. It's like I have a disease. Whenever I am home they seem to be gone. At least they don't leave any more booby traps behind. Maybe we're turning a corner."

"You were pretty steamed the night they dropped the bacon pail on your head. Maybe they're just afraid of you now. And after your accident, a little distance may not be a bad thing."

While Haden tried to relieve tensions between Wally and the Pruitt boys, Asmodeus took a different tack. The judge had become a regular presence at the Pruitt household, visiting for dinner, tea time, parties, chamber concerts, lectures, and any other reason Mrs. Pruitt could think up. The latest occasion was a garden party at which the wealthy and powerful of Mortania graced the Pruitt household. Even Mayor Daggot and his wife dropped by.

On that particular occasion, Wally tried to escape the house unseen, but got swept up by an effervescent Mrs. Pruitt.

"Wally, dearest," she said in her new, sugary style, "be so kind as to get the judge a drink."

Wally retrieved a glass of punch for Asmodeus, hoping he could hand it off and run.

"Why, thank you, Waljan," Asmodeus said. "Come, walk with me." Asmodeus put his arm around Wally and sauntered to a secluded corner of the garden, dragging Wally along. "So, how is that ankle of yours doing?"

"Fine, Your Honor, thanks for asking," Wally replied cautiously.

"You are lucky you're alive, you know. You did hear what happened to my officers."

"Last summer? Yes, Your Honor, I did. I am sorry for your loss."

Asmodeus looked amused. "I would like to know what you are doing about all the abuse you suffer here."

"I'm not sure what you mean."

Asmodeus searched for prying ears and, then satisfied, explained, "The Pruitt boys shouldn't get away with trying to murder their mother's lodger, depriving her of income and bringing scandal to the family name, don't you agree?"

"Murdering me?" Wally started to feel a little flutter in his stomach.

"At the Falls. Surely it was no accident." Asmodeus studied Wally's baffled expression. "Ahhh . . . you don't know what happened! You must not remember."

"Well, no," Wally said.

"And no one has told you, have they?"

Wally felt the heat rising in his neck and cheeks.

"You didn't fall into the river, Wally. You were pushed. You weren't supposed to be found by that Moriel fellow. The twins wanted you dead. My guess is they still do. You should make them pay for what they have done and stop them before they follow through."

Wally didn't trust Asmodeus's counsel, not so much for its content but for who was giving it. "Look, Your Honor, I don't want any more trouble with the Pruitts. Maybe it is better that we forget you brought this up."

"What would the King think about your cowardice?"

"What are you talking about?" Wally asked.

Asmodeus turned from concerned counselor to antagonist in a flash. "Oh, you are a thick one, Wally. Why the King of the Realm would want you in the Kingdom is beyond me, really," he replied.

"What do you know about it? I thought you didn't believe in the King," Wally responded.

"Ah, but you do," Asmodeus said. "Let's say for the sake of argument that I do as well." Asmodeus paused pensively, tapping his chin with his skull-tipped walking stick. Then he slipped right up into Wally's face.

"You have a problem. The King is watching you. And I don't think he likes what he sees. These two worthless Pruitts prey on innocent people. They cause embarrassment to their poor mother, they injure people. Sure, they leave you alone now that you are surrounded by protectors like Moriel. But they've just shifted their attention to less fortunate victims."

The judge backed off but held Wally's gaze. "They're a plague on our little town, and you would say, 'It's none of my business, I'll leave it alone.' Well, are not the people of Mortinburg the King's business? And isn't the King's business your business? But you are lazy. You are carefree. You want to make it to Abidan and enjoy the glories of the Realm without working for it . . . without making a difference for good here in Mortinburg." Asmodeus finished his speech and leaned back against a post, watching his words work their way into Wally's mind.

"I never really thought about it that way," Wally said, more to himself than to Asmodeus. He started to feel like he had missed something very important.

"I know," Asmodeus replied, handing Wally his empty punch glass. "Well, I have to be off. City business. Please give my apologies to Josephine." And he was gone.

21
The Best and the Worst

FIREWORKS colored the sky with flashes of yellow, red, and white. The night of the Jubilee had arrived. Wally had never experienced anything like this. To celebrate the founding of a city with friends, neighbors, and even strangers was a very special joy. For the first time since he had left the Wood, Wally felt like he really fit in here.

The day before, Wally had been bubbling over with excitement. He whistled through his work and could hardly stop talking about all the sights, sounds, and events planned for the celebration. Anyone who had anything to do with the preparations came into the store for supplies, and he was in the middle of it all. Haden, however, was unusually somber.

"Don't you like the Jubilee, Sir?" Wally asked.

"Oh, sure I do," Haden replied. "But it is times like these when we are distracted from what is most important. Be on your guard, Wally. The enemies of the King are always finding ways to trip us up. Noise, revelry, and mobs of people focused on a single idea have an odd and sometimes frightening effect on events. We just need to remember that, and everything will be fine."

"Well, I wasn't expecting it not to be fine until you brought it up, Sir," Wally replied.

Haden smiled. "Well, maybe I'm just getting too old and suspicious."

Mr. Constance interrupted. "Come on, gentleman! Enough chatter . . . we are going to be very busy today. It looks like I will be enjoying the festivities from here tomorrow. We better take lunch on our feet." A long line of customers was forming at the front desk. "Wally, take my keys and go get a bag of coins out of the safe. The register is running low."

"Yes, sir." Wally took the keys and made his way back to the vault. This was his chance. Sifting through the various baubles that hung from the ring, he found a little heart identical to Mrs. Pruitt's in everything but size. Cautiously, Wally cradled the gem in his hand.

A rush of crushing loneliness swallowed him up. All the joy and confidence he had recently lived was replaced with dark emptiness. His hands shook and he dropped the key chain. Like a piece of cork popping up from the black depths of the ocean, Wally's sadness vanished. There was no longer doubt about Asmodeus's gems.

Quickly, Wally picked up the ring, and, finding the right key, opened the vault. He grabbed a coin bag and returned to the floor.

"Haden, I need to talk to you."

"Mr. Constance is really on edge, Wally. I've never seen him like this. I really think we should focus on our work," Haden said. "We can talk later."

"But . . ."

"Wally!" Josiah Constance yelled from the register. "Where are those coins!"

"Coming, Mr. Constance!"

Customers continued to swarm in and out of the store throughout the remaining day. There was nothing Wally could do but wait for a chance to talk to Haden after hours.

As Wally prepared to leave for the evening, Haden yelled over to him from a delivery wagon that had just come in. "Boy! Good news from the Wood! The Longbows will be coming for the Jubilee tomorrow."

* * * * *

Haden and Wally ambled down Main Street amid the music and mayhem of Mortinburg's Centennial Jubilee. Despite his misgivings from the day before, Haden seemed just as delighted as Wally to enjoy a night at the festival. The warm, sweet smells of hot cider and pastries filled the air, and cheerful streamers hung between buildings. They passed a costumed man whose face was covered in blue paint, juggling three clay balls and a live chicken. The bird squawked and flapped hysterically. Rolling along on a log, two other men performed a mock sword fight. They shuffled past a parade of dancing ponies just in time to avoid the animals' high-stepping hoofs. Wally could have simply wandered and watched for hours, enjoying every moment.

"Do you see Peep anywhere, Sir?" Wally yelled over the commotion of the crowds.

"Not yet. But I think we should be looking for Cullie. There is no way we will spot Penelope in this crowd." It seemed to Haden that every living soul in Mortania had come.

They crossed the courtyard where Asmodeus stood on a platform at the base of the clock tower. He shouted pretty words toward the crowd, too long and fancy for Wally to understand. Soon, the entire town would gather for the ringing of the clock bells. Then, the mayor would be introduced.

"I will go over to the stables and see if Cullie's rig is parked there," Haden said. "They may have gotten a late start. I will meet you back at the clock tower when the mayor is done with his speech."

As the crowds congregated from all points, Wally hopped up on a fence post to get a good view. The mass of heads hemmed in around Wally, forcing him to stand up on the fence rungs. Mayor Daggot began his bluster and pomp.

Wally sat back down to wait it out. The speech went on far longer than he expected and he grew bored. His mind wandered. Yesterday's conversation with Haden mingled with Asmodeus's accusations of cowardice, and Wally suddenly felt antsy and restless. He decided to find some way of being useful while awaiting Haden's return.

Wally jumped off the fence and headed toward the edge of town. A group of children ran past him with various toys, trinkets, and noisemakers. Wally smiled at their innocent joy.

Presently, Wally noticed an orange haze rising above the Mercantile. Mr. Constance planned to keep the Mercantile open for the jubilee and watch the mayor's presentation from the second story. But the upper windows were dark. Wally expected the store was busier than Mr. Constance anticipated and that Wally's help would be appreciated.

Hands in his trouser pockets, Wally caught sight of a falling star as he crossed the street toward the store. If it weren't for Tyre Pruitt's "Watch out!" Wally would have plowed right into him as Tyre sprinted from the back of the Mercantile with Caddock at his heels. Just as Caddock passed Wally, the Mercantile lurched up in a violent explosion that catapulted wood and debris into the street and shot flames high in the air. The boys dropped to the ground. Allie shot out from under the walkway and disappeared down the street.

"What did you do?!" Wally screamed in Caddock's face. "What did you do; Mr. Constance is in there!"

Caddock sputtered and struggled but Wally would not wait for an answer. "Caddock, we can't leave him in there!" he insisted.

Tyre came running back in protest. "It's too late! Caddock, let's go!"

Wally ignored him and glared at Caddock. "Do you want to be responsible for Mr. Constance's death? Help me!"

Black smoke billowed out from where the door had blown off its hinges, and Wally knew they had to act quickly. Shouting out a rescue plan, he dragged Caddock up to the door of the Mercantile. They cowered against the intense heat.

"He was supposed to be upstairs," Wally explained. "But the lights are out. Just call to him. If he is in the store, he may be able to follow your voice."

Trying to get access to the upstairs window, Wally shimmied up a column onto the porch roof. The hot blaze raced through the store, catching quickly on wooden shelves, papers, and textiles, exploding boiling bottles of astringents and oils. Finally, the entire structure began to collapse and before Wally reached the window, the porch roof crashed down, throwing him to the street.

"Caddock!" Tyre screamed. He scrambled away for help, despite the fact that the explosion had already alarmed the entire city. People started to arrive with water buckets. But Wally knew it was too late. No one was coming out of that building now. Not Mr. Constance. Not Caddock Pruitt.

Two lines formed, one to provide a continual stream of water buckets for dowsing the fire, and another to hand the empty buckets back to the water silo for refill. The heat was so great that the water hardly made a difference. It just fizzled into a useless puff of steam.

Around them, but at a safer distance, the citizens and visitors looked on, some with their hands over their faces, others with their arms tightly folded across their chests, and several holding their children close. The tragedy seemed unbearably heavy as set against the gleeful sights and sounds not an hour before. No one was prepared for this. The flames produced a dry, painful wind that backed them farther away.

Mrs. Pruitt broke through the crowd, screaming her son's name. But Caddock could not hear her. He had climbed Castle Wall.

The decision was made to save the water stores. The building could not be saved, nor anyone inside. The people stood in quiet shock, as smoldering ash flitted about like morbid fireflies. The intense heat distorted the onlookers' view. In shock, Wally slowly rolled onto his knees and stared into the inferno.

"How did this happen?" Judge Asmodeus demanded as he pushed through the crowd to get a closer look and take control of the situation. Tyre Pruitt followed close behind, and then Mr. Constance.

Wally could not believe his eyes. "Mr. Constance!" he said, "You're alive!"

"Yes, he's alive," Asmodeus said harshly. "Did you expect

otherwise?"

"Well . . ." said Wally, "He was supposed to be . . ."

"Supposed to be?" Asmodeus insinuated. "What do you mean by that?"

"Nothing . . ." Wally insisted. "I mean . . ."

"Tell us what you know about this, Waljan. Speak up!" Mr. Constance demanded.

Tyre shouted, "He killed my brother!"

The people gasped. Haden and Moriel came forward to calm the crowd.

"No—he was helping me rescue Mr. Constance," Wally explained.

"That's a lie!" Tyre protested. "You forced him to go in there. I saw you!"

"It was your fault the Mercantile was burning in the first place!" Wally replied hotly.

"We had nothing to do with that fire!" Tyre argued.

Haden intervened, "Wally, did you see the boys light the fire?"

"They came running from behind the Mercantile just before the explosion," Wally explained.

"But Wally, did you actually see them light the fire?" he insisted.

"No . . . but . . . Sir, they are always causing trouble!" Wally said. "Everyone knows that. They are a plague on this town."

A shocked murmur came over the crowd. Haden's heart sank. Asmodeus smiled but not in a way that anyone would notice.

"Wally!" Mr. Constance chided. "How could you say such a thing? The Pruitts saved your life at the river. If it were not for them, no one would have found you half-drowned and unconscious."

Wally felt sick. Asmodeus told him the boys pushed him into the river. No one had told him that they saved him as well. Wally scanned the crowd, searching for some expression of understanding or sympathy. His eyes fell on a curly redhead. Peep stared back, in shock and horror, and then disappeared.

Tyre continued to defend his brother. "We were just on our way to the clock tower when we noticed a small fire. We ran for help, but Wally stopped us just as the building exploded."

"So, you mean to be judge, jury, and executioner, Wally?" Asmodeus accused loudly so that all could hear. Grumblings rose from the crowd.

"No!" Wally protested through tears of frustration, grief, and fear. "I didn't know the store would collapse, honest! I was trying to save Mr. Constance."

Haden hushed him. It was not the time to try to explain when everyone was so upset and already convinced of Wally's guilt.

"Yes, saving Mr. Constance. You've said that already. But Wally, as everyone can see, Mr. Constance is right here!" said Asmodeus.

If it were not for Haden, Moriel, and the other Abidanians, Wally might have been convicted on the spot. But as Asmodeus continued to influence the crowd with his overlong accusations, the Abidanians quietly surrounded Wally and eased him out of the town. It was clear that justice would not be served if Asmodeus had his way. Moriel and Haden stayed behind to reason with the town leaders. By the time Wally reached the Eastern Ridge, the crowds had dispersed, Mrs. Pruitt was taken home to bed, and a tense debate began over Wally's fate.

22
A Grim Plight

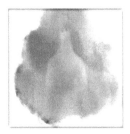

"HE'S gone!" A group of angry men, led by Bruce Malvo, gathered in the city center. Expecting that Wally had left town, they organized a search party that included Josiah Constance. Haden pulled his employer aside.

"Josiah. Do you really think Wally is capable of what he is accused of?"

"Judge Asmodeus seems to think so. That's good enough for me," Mr. Constance replied.

"The judge? Since when did the judge's opinions overrule what you know from your own experience?"

"Since he's tried to solve the increasing crime problem in this town. He's got my back, Haden. I thought you did too, but it seems to me that Waljan has been part of the problem Asmodeus is trying to fix. Maybe you were in on it? You and that brown-hooded vigilante friend of yours."

"Josiah! You and I have been friends a long time. You have watched Wally grow over the years I've had him in tow. How can you say these things?"

"I don't need an old woodsman and his murderous sidekick

154

hanging around my store. I have plenty of friends. And Asmodeus, the most important man in town, is the most trusted and generous among them."

"Is he, now? I would say he has a strange way of twisting things around."

"Say what you want, Haden. Wally's a plague on this town. And we're going to catch him."

"I've heard that expression one time too many, Josiah."

"If I still had the means to employ you, Haden, you would be fired. But as it is . . ." Mr. Constance let his words hang there and went to rejoin the group of thirty or so men.

Malvo surveyed the search party for a tracker. A tall young man came forward.

"I come from the Wood, officer. My dog and I can track just about anything, and I know the wild areas around Mortinburg well."

"What is your name, mister?" Malvo asked.

"Culbert Longbow, sir. I will need a little time to get my dog, Bo. But we'll make it up with his scenting skills."

"We'll wait. But make it quick," Malvo demanded.

Within an hour, Cullie returned to town with Bo Dog. He caught Haden's eye and offered a slight nod. Then, he proceeded to lead the party in the opposite direction that Wally had gone.

Haden had to piece together what had really happened that night. He was the only one who knew Wally's worst and best. And he knew that this entire misunderstanding represented both: Wally's tendency to hold on to grudges and his heroic heart. Waljan would suffer for both evil and good unless Haden could get to the truth. That truth lay with Tyre who, grief-stricken, would need a sympathetic ear and a shoulder to cry on.

* * * * *

Wally hadn't stopped running until he arrived at the Misting Pool, exhausted, alone, and defeated. His entire body shook. He was cold, but more so from shock than from the night air. He plunged himself into the pool and washed his hands and face so hard that his skin stung and turned red. It was as if he wanted to wash away the entire evening.

Wally waded out of the water and crumpled on the cavern floor. How could he have made such a mess of everything? How could he cause so much pain to so many people? He ached for Mrs. Pruitt and even for the twins. Moriel and Haden too must be ashamed of Wally. Poor Mr. Constance had lost everything. Worse, he believed he lost it all at the hands of a boy he had treated so kindly. Wally had thought he was doing something good. Now, he felt like a failure. Asmodeus won. The King would surely not want him now.

Sobbing deeply from the bottom of his heart, for all the hurt of a lifetime, Wally cried, "I wish Haden had never found me. Why did he have to find me in the Wood?"

A gentle weight pressed on his shoulder. Wally remained in a ball on the ground. Then the soothing lilt of Moriel's voice echoed through the chamber:

Our Regent wise, no good you spare
The children of your Kingdom fair
But should we stray, and turn away
The King waits in the mist.
His mercy's deep and Love will keep
He's waiting in the mist.

So when the pain of life has stained
Your heart coal black, the world disdained

No plight too grim, return to him
The King waits in the mist!
So gather in, too long it's been
The King waits in the mist!

A fog began to swirl around the room and condense above the pool. Moriel lifted Wally to his feet and wiped the boy's face with his sleeves.

"No plight too grim . . ." Moriel said. "Wait here."

After removing his scabbard, the Knight of the Realm entered the water. He stood with his head bowed, and raised his hands toward the mystical white cloud. And as Wally looked on, he thought he saw something hovering in the mist. The mist took on a form that laid what looked like hands on Moriel's head and then vanished as quickly as it formed. Wally rubbed his eyes. He was so tired he was afraid to believe what he saw. Moriel returned and looked at Wally curiously.

"What is the matter, Waljan?"

"I think I saw him! I saw the King!" Wally said.

"You are so surprised," Moriel mused. "Wally, your confession here was sincere. Why would the King sacrifice himself for those who betrayed him, but fail to forgive you? You, who so earnestly wants to please him? Haden found you because the King wished him to find you."

Then another familiar voice added, "And he thanks the King every day for having found you, Boy. You are the best thing that has ever happened to this old woodsman."

Wally turned to find Haden standing with Tyre at the entrance. A wave of remorse overtook Wally. Tyre stood with his arms hanging and shoulders slumped, his eyes swollen, red and empty.

Wally ran to them and embraced Tyre. "I am so sorry, Tyre. I just wanted to save Mr. Constance. I didn't know about the river—that you and Caddock . . . I didn't want Caddock to get hurt. It is all my fault. Can you forgive me?"

"There is nothing to forgive, Wally. It wasn't your fault," said Tyre.

Haden reached into his shirt pocket and pulled out an object wrapped in a handkerchief. He carefully pulled the edges of the handkerchief away revealing a round metal object. "Waljan, do you recognize this?"

Wally's blood ran cold. "Yes, Sir. That's the compass that Asmodeus offered me. It has the ruby I tried to tell you and Moriel about. Mrs. Pruitt has one, and Mr. Constance. Half the town could have one for all we know."

"That explains a lot," Haden said. "Josiah was acting very strange tonight. I'm sorry we didn't pay better attention, Wally. Asmodeus must have given this to Caddock and Tyre after you refused it."

"You were right, Wally," Tyre confessed. "We did set the fire. But not because we wanted to. The judge told us that you were plotting against us. We were so afraid of you, and I don't know why. Afraid and angry all the time."

Haden explained. "I have heard of this. Each gift contains a heart-shaped fire gem. Fire gems have strange properties. The judge uses them to control people by playing on their deepest fears and desires."

Tyre continued, "Asmodeus promised that as long as we obeyed him, he would keep you away from us. He said he would blame you for the fire as a way to protect us. Even if we'd wanted to refuse . . . well, those officers of his are always watching."

"Haden, throw that wretched thing into the Misting Pool." Moriel directed.

The compass hit the water and sank, sending a sulfuric, bubbling ooze to the surface of the water before petering out and dissipating.

"It's time," Moriel decided. "We'll gather the community and offer Wally the Mist Rite; we'll introduce Waljan to the King. I have no doubt that Wally saw His Majesty in the mist tonight. He will need the King's strength for the trials ahead of him."

Wally didn't like the sound of that. "What is going to happen to me, Haden?" he asked woefully.

"I wish I knew, Waljan," Haden answered.

"Nothing that the King finds you unworthy to suffer," Moriel added.

"Do I have to be handed over to the people of Mortinburg?" Wally wasn't sure he was ready for this test.

"Remember how much the King has suffered for his people," said Moriel. "You are one of those people, Wally. His call to all is a call to you. There is nothing to fear. What more can happen to you that has not already happened to him? He gave himself up willingly to the people, and they unjustly took his life. He did not deserve his fate. And yet, he lives. You would give yourself up less willingly and deserve your fate more. Yet, he wants you to live. Allowing you to suffer difficulties is his way of molding you into the kind of person who will rejoice with him in the Realm. The worst that can happen to you is that you will return home to your King. Trust him."

Then Moriel turned to Tyre. "And what do we do with you, Mr. Pruitt?"

Tyre looked worried. His eyes studied Haden's face for a sign of hope.

"I believe that Tyre should join us," Haden replied.

"I agree. But the time is not right," Moriel decided. "Does he know where he is?"

"Hardly. He was in a daze most of the way here," Haden replied.

Moriel was not certain Tyre could be trusted yet with the location of the cavern. Until the boy could be trained and accepted by the community, caution was needed.

"Blindfold him and return him to his home by way of the doctor. He will need care."

23
The King in the Mist

"I DON'T understand!" Wally objected. "Why bring me here to safety only to send me back?"

"For the sake of justice, Wally," Moriel said. "I hoped that by now you would understand this. Abidanians represent the King of the Realm. And so they must be truthful, loving, just, and forgiving. By these ways, the people of Mortinburg might come to believe in the King. We are not abandoning you to the whims of Mortinburg. We are giving them an opportunity to know the truth."

"But Moriel, Asmodeus has control of the town. There will be no justice. No truth. There will only be accusation and judgment. I am not going back! I never belonged there in the first place, and I don't belong here."

"Where do you belong, Wally?" Haden challenged. "Where is home? If you are so certain that the Wood is not your home and Mortinburg is not your home and the Abidan community is not your home then you must know where home is!"

Wally just stared at the floor, his arms tightly folded over his chest.

"Is it where there are no problems? Is it where everything is easy? Where there is only justice and love and peace? There is such a place, but not in Mortania! And the only way to get there is the King's way. Discipline. Sacrifice. Service."

Overwhelmed, Wally hid his face in his hands.

"Waljan," Moriel intervened, "you have a heart for justice, and a compassionate spirit. Do you really think this is all about you? You are not in this alone. All of us here are facing this injustice. So if you don't go back, what happens to Geez? What happens to Tyre? Haden? What happens to all those who risked their lives and reputations to bring you here safely and those who must continue to live under Asmodeus's oppression? This is our fight. This is the King's fight. We are not sending you back. We are returning together as a community, and standing together as a community."

"I'm scared, Moriel," Wally admitted.

"We know. We're scared, too. But Abidanians cannot serve the King by hiding."

Wally apologized. "I appreciate everything you have all done and are doing for me. I didn't mean to seem ungrateful."

"We understand, Wally. If the King didn't think you were worthy to fight this battle, he wouldn't have called you in the first place."

Moriel and Haden knew that Wally would need strength and wisdom to follow through and prove his innocence. Asmodeus agreed to a month's preparation for the trial. And so Moriel and The Twelve decided that Wally should meet with the King of the Realm and continue his training.

Moriel laid Wally's Spirit Sword out on a stone table in the Misting Chamber. Wally stared at the glimmering weapon, imagining what it might say if it had a voice. *Waljan of the Wood, you*

*are no hero. You are not worthy of a weapon like me. You are noth-
ing. You belong among the creatures of the wilderness.*

Moriel entered the chamber with more exuberance than Wally was in the mood for.

"Good morning, my young page! Ready for some training?"

"Yes, sir," Wally replied somberly.

"Oh Wally . . . you're going to need a bit more energy than that to defend yourself against this master swordsman! Are you well?"

"I'm fine. I just don't think I will ever be able to lift that Spirit Sword."

"Well, let's try anyway."

Moriel threw Wally a roughly hewn wooden sword, and they began. Attack. Block, counter. Thrust, block, kick. Attack, block, lunge. Over and over, as the hours passed.

Wally was unsteady, but Moriel encouraged him. "Very, good! You're getting better."

"But I'm still knocking myself off balance, Moriel. I'm afraid I might just trip over my own feet!"

"Yes, I noticed that," Moriel said. "As you block, you need to shift your weight from the lead foot by stepping into your opponent. Then you can follow through with your pommel, elbow, or a side kick to the head. But you need to be quick because you'll weaken the pressure on his blade and he can step back and dodge. You see? Let's try it."

Wally got back into position, and Moriel attacked with an over strike. Wally countered, leaning a little too hard into Moriel. His point hit the floor, and he tumbled over his shoulder into a heap on the floor.

"Perhaps it's time for a break," Moriel suggested.

After lunch, Haden quizzed Wally on the Promises of Knighthood. Then, firewood needed collecting, and meat for dinner brought in. Days of hard training, study, and chores ended in nights of relaxation around a glowing bonfire.

"Being here is almost like returning to Mortwood," Wally said one evening as he, Moriel, and Haden rested under the stars.

"Yes," Haden answered. "It is very peaceful."

Moriel filled the cool night air with the velvety tones of a wooden flute. While Haden fed the bonfire with glowing bits of stray log that escaped the shifting blaze, Wally watched the flames dance.

"Haden, did you know my mother?" Wally asked, finally.

"I'm sorry to say I did not. Or maybe I am not sorry to say. It seems to me that leaving a defenseless child in a dangerous forest is an inexcusably evil act," Haden said.

"We don't know the circumstances, Haden," Wally replied, quietly.

Moriel lowered his flute and looked over at Haden. "I would say the apprentice just taught the master a lesson."

Wally blushed. "I didn't mean to be disrespectful, Sir."

Haden smiled. "It is not disrespectful to speak the truth in love, Wally."

"I wonder what she was like. I would have liked to have had a mother. I mean, you are a wonderful guardian, Sir . . ."

"Wally, you don't have to explain. Boys need their mothers. I don't make a very good one."

Then Moriel said, "Wally, you do have a mother."

Wally's questioning eyes invited Moriel to continue.

"The Queen Mother," Moriel explained. "She watches over all of us."

"What is she like?" Wally asked.

"Beautiful, of course," Moriel answered. "Calm. Gentle. Powerful. That traitor Uriel is terrified of her. She is noble and everything the mother of a King should be. You can ask her anything. She will never turn you away."

"Why haven't I ever met her?" Wally asked, confused and a little hurt for not having heard about this Queen before now.

"She lives with the King in Abidan," said Moriel.

Haden reached into the chest pocket of his buckskin vest and pulled out an opalescent stone the size of Wally's palm. "Well, I was saving this as a gift for your Mist Rite. But now seems like a better time to give it to you," he said as he pressed it into Wally's hand.

The stone was warm and very smooth. Its cloudy white and pastel surface seemed to dance and twist, lit from within. Wally followed the swirling patterns with his finger.

"I've seen these before! Mrs. Pruitt and Mr. Guest have one just like this. And Moriel has a huge one that glows when you touch it. But I don't know anything about them except that Mrs. Pruitt warned me to stay away from them and anyone who uses them. What does it do?"

"It's an Abidanian Speaking Stone," Haden explained. "Through it we communicate with those in the Eternal Realm: those who have arrived from Mortinburg, the Queen Mother, and of course the King himself."

Wally sat up straight. "So, that's what I heard!"

Moriel and Haden looked puzzled.

"So I can talk to the King! And he can tell me what to do. . . .He can tell me what to do when I get back to Mortinburg!"

"Wally, the King can do anything," said Moriel. "He certainly doesn't need a Speaking Stone to do it. But for reasons difficult for us in Mortania to understand, he tends to guide us in quieter ways. Ways that take patience and a peaceful heart."

Haden continued, "But in times of great need, loneliness, gratitude, or joy, knowing that we are heard by the King is a great comfort and a very effective way to ask for help when we truly need it."

"But I heard a voice. At the Pruitts', remember, Moriel? I thought you had said something . . . when I first found the Speaking Stone in Mrs. Pruitt's desk drawer, I heard a voice. I heard it again after she knocked it out of my hand. 'Come back to me.' That's what it said."

Haden shot Moriel a sideways glance. Moriel nodded slowly as if receiving an idea in bits and pieces that he was just fitting together.

Wally caught their gradual realization. "What . . . ? Wait. Is Mrs. Pruitt an Abidanian?" The suggestion was ridiculous to Wally. Mrs. Pruitt was a good woman at heart. But she wasn't concerned with much beyond her own life and interests. And she was so friendly with Asmodeus who hated Abidanians. Wally rejected the idea the moment he mentioned it.

"She was, Wally," Haden replied. "Long ago. Her husband was a good friend. A Knight of the Realm. A hero. He was murdered a couple months before the twins were born. She could never come back to the community after that."

"He wants her back," Wally said and then waited for confirmation that never came. "Moriel, what are you not telling me?"

Moriel answered, "We don't know what this voice you've heard is or means, Wally. You have experienced something we can't explain. Only those faithful to the Realm can communicate through the Speaking Stone. And even then, not everyone can use it in the same way. Some experience the Realm with their senses, as if they were really there. But most people experience the Realm in subtle ways, through the community, the Edicts, events, or our own thoughts. Your perception is not typical."

"Have either of you ever seen the Realm?"

Moriel shook his head. "We see the King in the Mist as all true Abidanians do. But what you describe has not been our gift."

"I must be mistaken, then. I didn't hear anything. I mean, if you can't, how can I?" Wally examined the opalescent stone. "It's beautiful, anyway."

Haden encouraged him. "Boy, don't underestimate the power of the Speaking Stone. Or your heart."

The day leading up to Wally's Mist Rite was full of joy. Everyone pushed aside thoughts of Mortinburg and focused on the ceremony and celebration. Abidanian women had woven the customary ceremonial attire for Wally: a fine, white tunic of linen, pantaloons, and a blocky skull cap. Gladiola petals floated on the top of the pool and incense of thyme perfumed the cavern.

According to tradition, a great feast was prepared in the after chamber, and some of Wally's closer friends brought gifts for him. Moriel had purchased a scabbard lined with the wool of the finest sheep in Mortinburg for Wally's Spirit Sword. Wally would also receive a soft pouch on a silk lanyard to store his Speaking Stone, and a scroll of poetry, "The Ancient Deeds of the King of the Realm," which told of the adventures and history of Abidan.

But before he could enjoy the celebration, he first had to undergo the Mist Rite. The ceremony began by presenting Waljan of Mortwood, charge of Haden of the Realm, to the assembly.

He stood before them, wearing a rough woven sack.

"My friends!" announced the Abidanian curate. "Waljan of Mortwood has requested to know the King. Do you agree?"

"We agree!" cried the people.

The curate presented a ceremonial bowl where Wally washed before kneeling at the edge of the Misting Pool. There he stayed while the assembly chanted the Summoning. The mist thickened above the pool and a voice said, "Rise child of the dead. Live and greet the King."

Wally's stomach twinged, and he stood up, eyes fixed on the mist. He walked forward and raised his arms toward the skies. Closing his eyes, he breathed in the cool mist and everything around him faded away. The cavern was gone. The people were gone. He was alone in darkness, but he was not afraid. An overwhelming peace and joy seemed to fill him more completely than anything ever had before. It was like breathing in pure energy, filling his lungs, down into his toes, and up into his head. Soon, he noticed a bright light shimmering before him.

The light grew and a majestic figure appeared. His features were barely visible in the light. Wally could sense that he was powerful yet gentle, like love itself.

Strangely, as if a spark of imagination had escaped him and come to life, the land of Abidan emerged from the center of the light where the figure stood. Vibrant hues, more real than any Wally had ever seen, colored the vision. Teeming with the most graceful creatures, the landscape stretched before him. Trees full and bursting with fruit, fragrant flowers, and rippling meadows filled the land. In the distance, cascades tumbled into glittering rivers.

Wally felt as if he were looking at this place through a tunnel.

He knew there was much more to see, but he could barely take in what already lay before his eyes. And he didn't want the vision to end.

Around the King's head, points of light flitted. Wally didn't understand what they were, but they made him smile. As they darted about, they made a crystalline noise. Although nothing like the noises people make, he could only describe it later as singing.

Then he heard, "Welcome, Child of Abidan. I have been waiting for you."

He opened his eyes. Dazed by the sudden change of scene, Wally slowly realized he was still in the cavern, up to his knees in water. The mist was gone. Attendants stood around him. They led him behind a screen, where they prepared Wally for presentation. In crisp white linen, beaded sandals adorning his feet, and his sheath buckled securely around his waist, Wally approached Moriel on the speaker's platform.

Before him, Moriel knelt. Wally's Spirit Sword lay across Moriel's outstretched palms. This was the moment that Waljan would be judged worthy to serve the King. His doubts unnerved him. Tremors shot through his knees, and he tried to steady his hands.

Moriel's eyes, fixed solidly on Wally's, assured him, "You can do this."

Wally reached for the grip, and immediately felt the stubborn weight of it pulling him down. Wally clutched his Speaking Stone through the leather pouch that hung around his neck. *My King, I am yours if you will have me!* he thought. Then, as if the sword was set free from constraints, Wally lifted it high above his head in triumph.

Moriel announced, "Please welcome, Waljan of the Realm, Knight of the First Order!"

The cavern exploded in applause and cheers. Hours of joy, friendship, and revelry followed, hours he treasured forever. He had a family now, a community that supported him and loved him. Tomorrow would bring its troubles, but tonight he would celebrate.

24
Confessions

ASMODEUS surveyed the crowd like a hungry predator. A troop of Abidanians had risen early that morning to escort Waljan to trial. The judge spotted them and tracked the party with cold eyes from the edge of town into the center of the court. Wally did not understand what drove Asmodeus to appear so friendly one moment and so hateful the next.

Asmodeus set up the trial outdoors, by the blackened remains of the Mercantile. The judge's chair, higher than the hundreds it faced, sat between an accuser's booth and a defender's booth. The sight of Mr. Constance consoling Mrs. Pruitt in the accuser's booth stung Wally's heart. These two people had played important roles in his two years here. He couldn't bear their judgment against him.

Every seat in the audience was filled, but the people continued to file in. With a nod of his head, Haden called Moriel's attention to the soldiers at arms who lined the back and sides of the courtyard. Among them, Moriel recognized Malvo and Coleman.

"Since when did the Mortinburg town leaders hire soldiers for public trial?" Haden asked Moriel.

"Since they allowed Asmodeus to influence town policy, I imagine," Moriel replied.

"As we go into the court unarmed," said Haden.

"It is our custom. We must honor it, Haden."

Wally was astonished at the crowds. "All of Mortania must be here!"

"Word gets around. Many of these folks were at the jubilee, Wally," Moriel explained. "But don't worry. You have friends here."

Moriel and Wally set their Spirit Swords on a table among other citizens' weapons before taking their places in the defender's booth with Haden. Surly looking brutes guarded the weapons, ensuring that Asmodeus and his men would control any possible outcome of the trial.

Haden assessed the area, and then made a report. "Moriel, take a look at the wood pile over by the feed store. Someone left his ax. That'll do in a pinch."

Moriel reprimanded his friend. "Relax, old man. There isn't going to be a pinch. What has gotten into you?"

"A longing for justice," Haden replied.

As he waited for the proceedings to begin, Wally took note of all those in the audience whom he'd come to know. Some hoped for his demise, others for his release. Geez nodded to him and offered his fist in a gesture of support. Chaz Myrtle sat with his arms crossed, glaring at Asmodeus. Sitting next to Chaz was a man Wally did not expect to see, Culbert Longbow. But, where was Peep? He remembered seeing her the night of the fire, and his stomach lurched.

Oh no! She thinks I set the fire!

Asmodeus opened the proceedings with a summary of the charges. "Will the accused please stand and state his name."

Wally rose, preoccupied with thoughts of Peep, and pulling nervously at his white linen tunic. "I am Waljan of the Realm."

Asmodeus sneered. "Are you, now? No longer Wally Woodland?" He brushed dust from his top hat and adjusted it on his head with a bit of a tilt. Then he took a long look at Wally, still dressed in his Mist Rite finery. "Well, I guess that explains why you wore that ridiculous costume to these proceedings."

A hum of voices and quiet sniggers issued from the crowd. Wally blushed. But then, Geez shouted from among them, "So, what's your excuse, judge?" Robust laughter overtook the audience.

"Who said that?!" Asmodeus wheeled around and slammed the butt of his walking stick on the floor. "Disruptions will not be tolerated!"

The crowd abruptly settled down.

"So, it's 'Waljan of the Realm,' is it? After what you've done, I don't blame you for changing your name. No doubt this is your doing, Moriel. Should we have questioned whether the boy is mentally fit for a trial? He seems to be all too willing to believe in your fairy tales."

"The boy can speak for himself, Your Honor." Moriel replied.

"Very well." Asmodeus took a deep breath and began. "Vengeance and envy. Vengeance for a few harmless pranks and envy for the loving home an angry orphan could never call his own. Vengeance and envy have deprived a man his livelihood and ourselves the benefit of his products and services at the Mortinburg Mercantile. It lies here in ruin as you all can see. But far worse, they have deprived a beloved son and a cherished member of our community his very life."

Mrs. Pruitt began to wail pitifully, held by Josiah Constance.

Asmodeus continued, "Waljan Woodland of Mortwood, or the Realm, whichever you prefer, is an ungrateful and angry soul, who must be punished for the damage he's done."

Over the next hour the judge proceeded to paint a verbal portrait that bore little likeness to the real Wally. Every word found agreement among many there. Finally, he wrapped up his comments.

"Waljan was so consumed with rage that he cared more for vengeance than for the employer who treated him so well, for the mother who opened her home, for the life of a peer. We were all there. We are all witnesses to the events that evening. This trial is merely an obligation to justice, a matter not of whether one is guilty, but what should be done about it."

At this point, Asmodeus had successfully persuaded even those who had arrived at the trial undecided. But he wasn't finished. He called forward Tyre Pruitt.

"Tell the good people, Mr. Pruitt, what happened that night," Asmodeus said.

"Well, you know what happened as well as I do," Tyre responded.

"For the sake of justice, Tyre. Please, don't be afraid," Asmodeus replied.

Before Asmodeus realized what was happening, Tyre said, "Well, Your Honor, you'd been working on Caddock and me for a while. I admit we were the kind that enjoyed getting into a bit of trouble. But we never would have really hurt anybody if you hadn't scared us with your stories of Wally's vengeance and then threatened us into cooperating. I don't know what you have against Waljan, but you certainly played Caddock and me."

"Mr. Pruitt! I am warning you. Tell the truth and stop playing these games. This is serious city business!" Asmodeus scolded.

Mrs. Pruitt, who had come to trust Asmodeus entirely, also interjected, "Tyre! Stop this! How dare you treat the judge this way? He has been our most loyal and generous friend."

Tyre looked sorrowfully at his mother who fingered the fire gem at her throat. He continued, now addressing the audience directly. "Asmodeus warned us that only as long as we did exactly what he said could he protect us. So, on the night of the fire . . ."

"Enough!" Asmodeus shouted. "I have had quite enough of you!"

With a flick of his hand, Asmodeus directed Malvo and Coleman to pull Tyre from the witness chair. Mrs. Pruitt screamed. Mr. Constance jumped to his feet. But it was Alicia who impulsively shot forward from the crowd, her wild hair flying about.

"Leave him alone!" she screamed. "Leave us all alone, you wicked man!"

Realizing her mistake, Allie stopped cold in the middle of the proceedings like a frightened rabbit. Asmodeus rose and descended his perch.

"Oh, what is this town coming to? You see, my dear people? Everything is turned around. Now we have the village witch defending her own. Defending the troublemakers, the riffraff, the criminals. Need I say anything more?"

He circled Allie, who felt vulnerable and exposed, gawked at by everyone in the crowd. He taunted her loudly. "This thing. Now the full truth comes out for all to know."

Allie tried to get away from Asmodeus, but he grabbed her by the arm.

"Let me go!" she cried. "Haven't you done enough? Haven't you caused enough pain?" Allie hid her dirt-streaked face.

Asmodeus ignored her. "Waljan of the Realm? Knight of Abidan, I suppose? No, not a knight at all. We know better, don't we Allie . . . or should I call you Alicia? Alicia of Mortwood, wasn't it? The mother of this criminal, Waljan. Oh, and she was a beauty once, my friends. Hard to see it, now. She and her husband, him long dead from reckless living, abandoned Waljan as a baby. He was too wretched even for them."

"No!" Allie looked up at Waljan. "He is a liar! He took you from me. . . ."

But Asmodeus barreled on, loudly. "This is the kind to which our criminal Waljan belongs. This worthless . . ."

Allie ripped herself free and jumped on Asmodeus with beastly fury. He struggled, throwing her off him. She fell in a heap on the ground. "This is the last time you assault me, shrew!" He advanced on her, lifting his walking stick.

Leaping out of the defender's booth, Waljan ran toward the weapons cache. Before the guards realized what was happening, Wally hurdled the table, grasped his Spirit Sword from the pile, and whipped the scabbard to the ground. He raced to the center of the courtyard. Before Asmodeus could bring his stick down over Allie, Wally blocked it with a slice from his sword, splintering the judge's shiny black stick into flying shards.

Asmodeus stumbled back on his heels as the crowd gasped. A gang of forces came running toward Wally, but Asmodeus raised his hand, and they halted like well-trained guard dogs. Then, he began to laugh with such a sinister air that Wally felt suddenly small and defenseless.

"Do you really think that you have any power here?" Asmodeus asked Waljan. "This is my town!" Then, he addressed the whole crowd. "Did I not warn you of the threat hidden among you? Are the myths you tell your children so innocent? Harmless? This boy and his foolish band skulk in the wilderness, plotting against their own people. They have weapons and serve an imaginary King!"

"He is not imaginary!" Wally blurted.

Asmodeus fixed his predatory eyes on Wally. "So. You admit your plot. First Mortinburg, then all of Mortania. The House of Uriel rules this world, child. My dear citizens! Do you hear this traitor's treachery? Do you want your families and neighbors threatened by these dangerous, mad Abidanians? To your feet! Defend your city!"

At that very moment, everyone's attention turned to a "THUNK! Thwop, thwop, THUNK!" The brutes surrounding the weapons cache dropped to the ground. From the clock tower a small redheaded figure yelled, "Long live the King of Abidan!"

"Peep!" Wally yelled, and then repeated her cry, "Long live the King of Abidan!"

Scores of Abidanians echoed, "Long live the King of Abidan!" and scrambled for their weapons. Chaz Myrtle, who was seated closest to the weapons cache, grabbed Paraclete and tossed her to Moriel. The audience panicked and frantically dispersed. But Asmodeus's soldiers drew swords and advanced on Wally. Each was met on the way by one of The Twelve and the Knights of the Realm.

"Well," Haden said to Moriel, "how's that for a pinch?"

"It will do!" Moriel cried and ran into battle.

Malvo and Coleman headed straight for Wally. But Haden still had enough fight in his old bones to join the fray by Wally's side. He grabbed the ax he spied at the beginning of the trial and swung it just in time to stop Coleman from attacking Wally from behind. Malvo waved a small knife at Wally's face, slicing and jabbing, searching for an opening around Wally's Spirit Sword like a crazed wasp.

From behind the accuser's booth, Asmodeus skirted the battle, shouting orders to his men. As the fighting turned decidedly against them, he slipped out of sight. By the time it was over, Asmodeus had fled with a third of the town, abandoning what was left of his defeated men.

Cullie, Chaz, and a band of young Abidanians searched the town and made a report to Moriel. "Sir, there is no sign of them anywhere. They have left town. We can try to pursue them if you wish."

"No, I think we have enough work to do here with casualties and establishing some order. We haven't seen the last of the judge, I can promise you that. See if you can find Mayor Daggot."

The townsfolk peered out from behind curtains and through cracked doors. Cautiously, some returned to tend to the wounded. Others assisted in rounding up those who had surrendered.

Wally sheathed his sword and ran to his mother's side. "Allie . . . Mother . . . are you okay?"

She smiled back at him. "It is you! I knew it was you! I see Aimas in those eyes. He told me you had died. I didn't want to believe him but I was so ill. Then you came to town with that hunter and from around corners I watched you grow. I was so ashamed;

I couldn't let you know. Forgive me. There was nothing I could do. I never wanted to leave you."

"Of course, Mother, I know. Everything is going to be okay," Wally replied. He raised his voice so that all in the square could hear, "We have all been deceived. Asmodeus is a dangerous coward, who takes joy in the pain of others. No one is too noble nor too low to attract his malice. He may be defeated today, but he still lives. Now that you know him, beware."

Wally stood and looked to Moriel, who nodded his approval.

"I am Waljan of the Realm, a Knight of the First Order of Abidan. I have seen the King. He too is alive and waits for all who desire their rightful home, the Kingdom of Abidan. All Glory to the King of the Realm!"

Then he turned back to Allie. "Please let me help you, Mother."

Haden appeared by his side. "Take her to the cavern, Waljan," he suggested. "Go quickly. Maggie's unhitched by the clock tower."

Wally nodded and helped Allie to her feet. "Come, Mother, Abidan awaits your return."

25
Mist and Mercy

STILL just a boy, but looking more like a man every minute, Wally picked up his mother and carried her off to the Eastern Ridge Falls. Most of the way she slipped wearily in and out of consciousness. She had been sick a long time. Alicia never fully recovered her health after leaving Wally. The grief of losing him and years of hard living had taken an additional toll. Now reunited with her son, she could let the world go.

But Wally could not let her go. He brought her to the Misting Pool and laid her at the water's edge. Gently, he scooped the sacred water over her forehead and hair. Years of dust traveled down in rivulets from her face and into the pool. Alicia opened her eyes, which still held a spark of the woman she once was, and stared into her son's.

"I am so proud of you! Maybe it was best that I left you. You have become such a courageous and strong young man," she said.

"I don't feel strong, Mother. And I missed you. I never really knew how much until now. I'm so sorry. I'm sorry I treated you as I did."

A group of ladies, healers among the Abidanians, filed through the tunnel with attendants and approached the two.

They convinced Wally to allow them to care for her. A small side chamber was prepared with a clean bed of straw and linens. The assistants bathed Alicia. They washed and combed her hair, anointed her with fragrant oils, and dressed her in clean robes. A roaring fire and healing broth warmed her. But nothing would undo all the damage she had borne through the years.

Wally waited at the pool until the attendants returned for him. "She wants to see you, Waljan."

He forced a smile as he approached the fragile, worn soul. A deep love replaced the loathing he once felt for her. In the Abidanians' care she had regained her humanity, but she looked like a lost child.

"Mother, don't be afraid. Everything is going to be all right now," Wally said.

Alicia replied, "I have heard of the King. Asmodeus often belittled those who spoke of him. You called yourself a Knight of the Realm. So he is real?"

"Yes, Mother. He is real. I will introduce you."

"No!" Alicia rose slightly and shook her head frantically. "No. I am not worthy of such a King. You don't know, Wally. The things I have done no one can forgive."

"If he is so great a king, what would stop him, Mother?" Wally reasoned. "Even Asmodeus would find refuge in Abidan if he changed his heart and asked sincerely. The King suffered torments to open Abidan to all who wished to return. Why would he deny anyone that chance now?"

Alicia smiled and lay back down. "I will sleep now." She grabbed Wally's hand and kissed it softly. "Waljan. Welcome home."

Haden and Moriel, having just arrived from town, entered the room. Seeing Alicia's condition, they gently eased Wally away from her side. Wally ran back to the pool. He reached into his shirt and pulled out the pouch that hung around his neck. Tearing at the drawstrings and turning the pouch over, Wally dropped the opalescent Speaking Stone into his hand. He rubbed it gently, rocking back and forth, and with all his heart poured out a plea for mercy.

"Please, Almighty King, don't take Alicia from me now. You can heal her somehow." He closed his eyes.

"Wally." Haden sat down next to him. "This is the land of the dead. Alicia has suffered so much. Isn't it time she be allowed to feel joy again? Don't you want your mother to be the woman she was meant to be? Happy? Free? Loved? Let her go. You of all people should know how much she needs to go home."

Wally looked up at Haden tearfully and nodded. Haden held him until the pain of losing Alicia eased. As they stood to make their way out of the cavern, a mist developed over the pool. It was the first time Haden had ever seen a mist gather without the Summoning Chant. Moriel joined them in their astonishment, as a faint image of a beautiful young woman grew brighter and hovered above the pool. The woman was graceful, with a circlet of stars on her head and a royal cloak as blue as midnight about her shoulders.

The three dropped to their knees. No one had seen the Queen Mother before now.

"Waljan of the Realm," she called. "Someone has approached the Gates of Abidan. She speaks of you."

"Yes, my Lady!" Wally whispered in astonishment. "May I see her?"

"I am afraid not, Dear One. She is in the Place of Preparation. She is not yet ready to enter our courtyards. But soon. With your Speaking Stone you can comfort her and hasten her preparation. Don't worry. She is full of the joy of anticipation. She looks forward to seeing you when your work in Mortania is done."

"My work, Queen Mother?" Wally asked.

"You have much to do in service of the King, Dear One. Alicia is watching. And she is so proud of you. You have done well, my son." And the mist dissipated silently.

Wally turned to his friends, "Alicia has climbed Castle Wall."

"It is hard, Waljan. But it is good," Haden said.

Wally hoped to see Alicia again and come to know her as a sister of the Realm. But until that day, he resolved to serve the King well. At this moment, everything was just as it should be.

Acknowledgments

I would like to thank my family
for their love, support, and encouragement for this project,
particularly: my husband, Todd,
who never fails to celebrate my creative pursuits;
my daughter and cheerleader, Arielle,
who is always ready to lend a hand
and whose detail orientation rivals the best
of professional editors';
and my sister, Kim,
who has been a source of linguistic
and literary inspiration my entire life
and without whom I would have never attempted
to write anything other than a shopping list.

24 23 22 21 20 19   2 3 4 5 6 7 8 9

ISBN: 978-1-68192-527-1 (Inventory No. T2416)
LCCN: 2019939979

Copyedited by Nancee Adams-Taylor
Edited by Jerry Windley-Daoust
Designed and built by Steve Nagel
Cover illustrated by Susan A. Howard
Interior illustrated by Aaron W. Howard
Proofed by Karen Lynn Carter

Our Sunday Visitor Publishing Division
Our Sunday Visitor, Inc.
200 Noll Plaza
Huntington, IN 46750
1-800-348-2440